The Crow-Girl

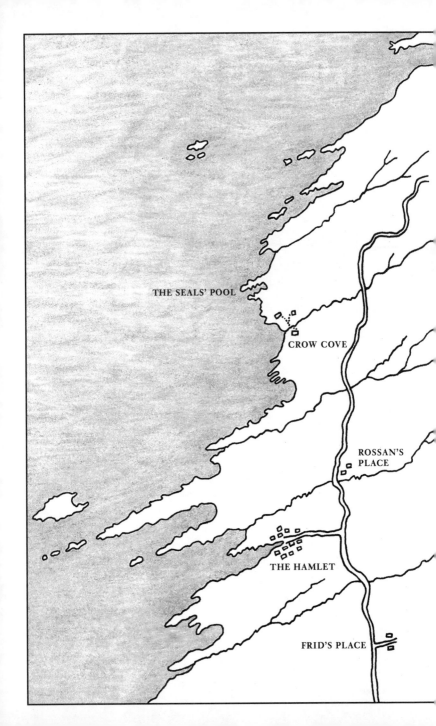

THE SEALS' POOL

CROW COVE

ROSSAN'S
PLACE

THE HAMLET

FRID'S PLACE

The Crow-Girl

THE CHILDREN OF CROW COVE

Bodil Bredsdorff

Translated from the Danish by Faith Ingwersen

Farrar Straus Giroux ⋆ New York

Text copyright © 1993 by Bodil Bredsdorff
English translation copyright © 2004 by Farrar, Straus and Giroux
Originally published in Danish by Høst & Søn under the
title *Krageungen: Børnene i Kragevig 1*
Published in agreement with Høst & Søn represented by
ICBS, Copenhagen
Distributed in Canada by Douglas & McIntyre Ltd.
Printed in the United States of America
Designed by Nancy Goldenberg
Map designed by Bodil Bredsdorff and Nancy Goldenberg
First edition, 2004
1 3 5 7 9 10 8 6 4 2

www.fsgkidsbooks.com

Library of Congress Cataloging-in-Publication Data
Bredsdorff, Bodil.
    [Krageungen. English.]
    The Crow-girl / Bodil Bredsdorff ; translated from the Danish by
Faith Ingwersen.— 1st ed.
        p. cm.
    Summary: After the death of her grandmother, an orphaned young girl
leaves her house by the cove and begins a journey which leads her to
people and experiences that exemplify the wisdom her grandmother
had shared with her.
    ISBN 0-374-31247-8
    [1. Orphans—Fiction.   2. Conduct of life—Fiction.   3. Family
life—Fiction.   4. Grandmothers—Fiction.]   I. Ingwersen, Faith.
II. Title.

PZ7.B74814Cr 2004
[Fic]—dc22

                                                                    2003049310

The English translation was supported by the Literature Centre at Danish Arts.

The Crow-Girl

1

Near a little cove where a brook ran out to the sea stood three houses. One of them was not really a house anymore. It was a ruin, with only the lowest part of the walls still standing.

The second house was in better shape, but it was also unoccupied. There were holes in the roof, and rain and wind had scoured off the whitewash, so you could see the gray stone it was made of.

The third house was all the way down by the sea. It was white with a chimney at each gable, and in it lived a young girl and her grandmother.

The cove was completely quiet except for the

brook's gurgling and the sound on the narrow shore of pebbles being driven back and forth across the rocky ground by the swells. An eagle let itself be carried by the wind out across the water. A wisp of smoke was rising from one of the chimneys.

Inside the house the girl was stoking up the embers on the hearth. She dug them out from beneath the ashes, laid dry twigs of heather across them, and blew and blew until the fire caught and clear little flames brightened her face.

Her eyes were dark blue, nearly black in the dim light. She had a large curved nose and dark, bristly hair that was very short in front where the fire had singed it.

As the fire crackled in the heather, the girl added large pieces of firewood, driftwood smooth as silk and bleached gray by the sea.

"You're taking the old pieces, aren't you?" said a voice from the settle's pull-out bed.

"Yes, of course," said the girl.

"Because you know if it's too fresh, there'll be tarry soot in the chimney."

The old woman coughed a bit and turned over. "It's all that salt in it. And tarry soot smells bad."

"It's all right, Grandmother," the girl said to calm her. "It's lain over behind the house for the last half year, so rain has washed out all the salt."

"That's good, my chick. Come! Give me your hand!"

The girl sat down on the chair beside the settle bed and put her hand in the old woman's.

"Tell me how my hand feels," her grandmother said.

The girl wrapped her fingers around it and thought a moment. "It's warm and dry," she said. "And, in a way, smooth, even if it's wrinkled. A bit like driftwood."

"Can you move it?" asked the grandmother.

The girl gently bent the old woman's fingers and then straightened them out again. "Like that?" she asked.

"Exactly," said her grandmother. Then she cleared her throat, and because she did so, she began coughing again. When she stopped, her voice was a little stronger, and she said, "If I'm lying here completely still one day and don't answer you, take my hand and feel it. If it's cold and stiff and you can't move it, it will be because I'm dead."

The girl remained silent, squeezing the old woman's hand tightly and wishing that those words had never been spoken. Outside, it was about to grow dark. The fire crackled, and its light made the shadows in the room dance on the whitewashed walls. The two didn't move for a long time.

"I had better make dinner," said the girl finally, and pulled her hand back.

The old woman had fallen asleep.

The fire was warming things up, yes, warming nearly too much if one got too close. The girl brought in the basket of mussels, which she had left on the bench outside the house. She had walked in cold water for several hours to gather them from the rocks. Afterward, she had scrubbed them in the brook.

Now, one by one, she carefully tapped them against the rim of the pot. If they still did not close their shells completely, she threw them outside the door. The seagulls would carry them away when it grew light.

Then she hung the pot on the hook above the fire and poured in a little water. When it boiled, she tipped the mussels down into the pot, put the lid on, and waited for a short while. When the pot was steaming, she took it off the fire, lifted the lid, and this time threw out the mussels that had not opened up.

There was the sound of a cough from the settle bed. Her grandmother had awakened again.

"Have you sorted them?" asked the old woman.

"Yes," said the girl, "both before and after I boiled them."

"A person can get sick from mussels if they are tainted. Then they are like pure poison. But when they are good, you can't find anything better."

The girl divided the mussels into two bowls and poured water from the pot over them.

There was no need for spoons, since each mussel lay in its shell and, along with a little of the broth, was easily scooped up.

The old woman ate a couple, then handed the bowl to the girl. "Here, my chick, you take the rest."

"Aren't you going to have any more?" asked the girl, astonished. She knew that this was her grandmother's favorite food.

The old woman shook her head. "When you don't move about, you don't need so much," she said.

When the girl had eaten all the mussels, she was still hungry, but she didn't say so.

"Take all the shells, pour water over them, and boil them one more time," said the old woman. "It makes a good, warming drink. Why don't you give me a mug of it, too?"

As they sat, each with her own mug, the old woman on the settle bed and the girl on the chair, the grandmother began to speak:

"You will find two kinds of people in the world. Some say that there are the bad and the good. But it isn't like that. Since what is good for one may be bad for another. No, that doesn't work. You have to depend on your intuition.

"There are those who make you feel inside as if you are drinking a good, warm soup—even if you are hungry and the two of you have nothing to eat. In spite of that they nourish you.

"And then there are those who cause you to freeze inside, even if you are sitting before a roaring fire and have eaten your fill. Those you should keep away from. They are not good for you, even though others might say that they are good people. Remember that, my chick."

The girl nodded.

"That's the first rule. Then there's the second, but I'll wait until I'm lying down again to tell you."

The girl helped her remove the pillows behind her back. The old woman began coughing when she lay down.

"Maybe you should give me a couple of them after all. It'll be easier for me to catch my breath."

And the girl placed two pillows under her grandmother's head.

"I'm tired now," said the old woman. "I'll tell you about the second rule in the morning. You had better go to bed, too. You've had a long day."

The girl took a hide, rolled it out on the floor before the hearth, and then pulled another one over her. She lay for a while looking into the embers, which stirred as if they were living and breathing.

"Don't lie too close to the fire," she heard from the settle bed. "You know how a spark can fly."

"Yes, Grandmother," said the girl.

They lay there again for a short while.

"You'd better bank the fire now," her grandmother said.

And the girl rose and scooped ashes on the coals so they would last until the next day. The room grew completely dark. There was a rustling from the settle bed.

"Grandmother," the girl said.

"Mmm," mumbled the old woman.

"Are you too tired to tell me about the North Star?"

"No, but I'll make it short," answered the old woman. "Can you remember your grandfather?"

"I best remember when we buried him."

"Oh, but before he died, he said to me, 'Once I am dead and you want to say hello to me, look up at the North Star; then I'll wink at you.'"

"Does he?"

"You can see for yourself."

"When you die, will you wink at me, too?" asked the girl.

"You'd better believe I will, my chick. But it won't be tonight, and now you should go to sleep."

The girl pulled the hide all the way up to her ears, so only her eyes peeked out, and she lay staring into the darkness. Then she saw a tiny coal winking at her from the ashes in the fireplace. Like a little star in the night sky. She thought about whether it might not be better to cover it. But before she managed to do so, she had fallen asleep.

2

A couple of days later it rained—a fine drizzle that drifted in from the sea, leaving beads of water on the blades of grass and making one's skin cold.

The girl had gone out to gather driftwood. But it had been a long time since a big storm had passed through, so not much wood was to be had. She decided to go farther down the shore to take a look at the sea kale.

She put the bits of wood she had found in a pile, drew her shawl up about her head, and tucked the empty basket under her arm.

The sea kale grew near an area with a lot of seaweed. The girl used the seaweed to cover the plants, and when they pushed up through the darkness, their stalks were white and crisp.

She took her knife from her belt and dug into a clump of seaweed, and there, at the very bottom, some small pale shoots of sea kale stuck up from the sand like birds' bones.

She brushed all the seaweed to one side and dug away the sand. The stems beneath were, in fact, much longer than the parts sticking up aboveground. But she was careful to leave a part of the plant. And she did not cover it up again. Now it had to gather strength until it could be forced again.

She took a couple more plants; the rest she let be, for it was always good to have a reserve supply to eat from. Then she put the basket down and walked along the shoreline over to some rocks that reached out into the water like a gnarled hand with many fingers. The cracks and clefts were teeming with small dark sea snails.

She began filling her cloth bag with snails. There was not much food from such small creatures, but they were quite pleasant to eat. It took such a delightfully long time. You could dig them out of their shells with a pin when they had been cooked.

The ebb tide had left several pools of water that would be cut off from the sea for a while. In one of them a little fish had been trapped. The girl speared it with her knife, cut open its belly, and cleaned it.

Immediately a couple of gulls flapped above her head, waiting for her to move so they could get their share.

The rain had forced its way through her clothes, but she had not noticed it. Now she began to freeze and hurriedly put the fish in the basket so she could go home.

Their house had two rooms, with a hall between them. One room they used as a larder and for storage. There, the girl emptied the basket before she went back out in the rain to get the driftwood she had collected.

She put it behind the house, farthest back in the row, so she could distinguish the new from the old. Then she went over to the other end and took a couple of pieces with her into the house, so they could dry out before they were to be used.

It was pleasantly warm in the main room. And completely silent.

"Grandmother," she called.

No one answered.

She ran over to the settle bed and grabbed the old woman's hand. It felt warm and dry and soft.

"I must have dozed off for a bit," said her grandmother, pushing herself up. "Well, my chick, did you find anything?"

And the girl happily told her about all her discoveries.

"You can feed a whole family," said the old woman, and patted her hand.

"A very little family," said the girl. "It can't be any smaller because then it would no longer be a family."

She immediately regretted what she had said, since her grandmother replied, "Indeed, whatever is going to happen to you? If only I had a place to send you, but I don't know anyone anymore."

"I can manage on my own. I can feed a whole family, you know—if there are only two," said the girl, laughing, even though she did not feel happy inside.

"Yes, of course, little one, that you probably can, but a person needs more than food. Even though it is nice to think that you can obtain food for yourself. In fact, you're really good at it."

"What shall I do with the fish? I had planned to put it in the clay fish-mold and roast it in the ashes, but we don't have anything to grease the mold with."

"That mold is so old and greasy that nothing can stick to it anymore. Just go ahead and use it." Then the old woman leaned back against the pillows, while a hoarse cough shook her body.

Soon afterward the attack subsided, and it grew quiet in the room.

"Listen," said the old woman a few minutes later. "There's a big storm approaching, so there will be timber coming ashore."

The wind slammed down the chimney and for a moment filled the room with smoke.

"Put more wood on, so the air in the chimney will be warm. Then that won't happen again."

The girl did as the old woman said.

———

"Now I will tell you the second rule," said her grandmother when they had eaten the fish and the sea kale. "I feel quite well. It's probably from all that good food you brought."

The girl had noticed that the old woman had eaten scarcely anything, but she did not say so and got up only in order to seat herself on the chair beside the settle bed.

"You just sit there in front of the fire where it's comfy, and eat your snails," said her grandmother. Then she cleared her throat. "The second rule says that the door to a person's heart can only be opened from within. If there is someone who will not let you in, it's no use hammering and kicking and lamenting and complaining. For what if the door is ajar, and you push it shut? With some people it can never be opened again."

The coughing returned, and the old woman stopped talking.

The girl finished the snails and sat looking into the flames, which were licking up along the sooty wood. The wind soughed out across the roof and shook the chimney, but did not come down it again.

"What else?" the girl asked.

"My word, I don't know why I'm telling you this. Maybe it's something that you have to experience yourself. Maybe a person travels more easily through life without having all those words to carry along."

"Yes, but I would like to hear it," the girl protested.

"Well, all right, my chick, but now I think I must rest a bit."

While the old woman dozed off again, the girl got up, cleared away the dishes, and laid more wood on the fire. A mouse scurried along the wall and disappeared into the darkness. The girl made her bed before the fire and was just about to lie down when the old woman began to speak:

"Then there is the third and most important rule. It's about a person's need to continue wishing and hoping, for then, at last, you will get what was wished and hoped for—even if it is in a completely different way from what you had imagined."

The house grew quiet again except for the wind on the roof and the fire's crackling. The girl remained sitting, staring into the flames. The only thing she wished and hoped for just now was that her grandmother would never get older, never die, never leave her all alone in the world. But how that wish would be fulfilled, she could not imagine.

In the flames there was no answer, only movement—movement and warmth, warmth and light. She continued to stare into them until everything grew quiet within her and time no longer existed.

3

It rained for many days, but early one morning the whitewashed walls were tinged a slight pink by the sun, which was about to rise. The girl stole carefully out of bed in order not to wake her grandmother. Then she slipped out the door and ran down to the brook.

The sun had just escaped the crest of the ridge. With a single little cloud as a faithful companion, it quickly changed colors, from red to orange to yellow, and ended in a piercing white. The light brought out the colors in the landscape and made the grass an even deeper green.

The sea lay blue and calm, gurgling against the rocks and pebbles on the shore. The brook murmured on its unending way to the sea. The girl sat down on a flat rock jutting out into the brook and looked at the flowing water. Then she stuck her hand into the water, cupping it slightly, and took a mouthful.

A black figure appeared in silhouette on the crest of the hill. The girl shaded her eyes with her hand and could see that it was one of the wild goats that had ventured out to the cove. With large twisted horns it was standing completely still, looking down at her. Suddenly it turned about with a start and disappeared behind the rocks.

The girl got up and walked along the shore to a place where two rows of rocks stretched out into the sea like long arms, forming a pool between them. She sat down on the bank and looked at the seals sunning themselves at the end of one of the reefs, which cupped itself like a hand dipping into the water.

The seals had seen her and raised their heads. One bellied its way down to the water and out into the pool and swam nearly all the way over to her. It positioned itself upright in the water and looked at her, its great dark round eyes peering directly into hers. That lasted a long time; the girl thought it seemed like an eternity. Then the seal turned around and swam back again.

The girl remained sitting, filled with the feeling that this was where she belonged, this was home. Here by the water and rocks and grass, the goats, seals, circling eagles, and screeching gulls.

After a while she got up and headed back to the house. In the larder she dug out a little tin that she had hidden a long time ago. There was a bit of tea left in it, and they were going to have it this very morning because it was such a lovely day.

She slipped into the main room, rolled up the hides, and put them away. Next she lit a fire on the hearth and hung a kettle of water up over the fire. When the kettle boiled, she took it down and poured the tea leaves into the water.

Sugar! Wasn't there also a bit of sugar someplace? She scurried back into the larder, where she rustled around like a mouse, until she found another tin with some sugar at the bottom. If only they had milk, too, how happy Grandmother would be. Scalding hot tea with milk and sugar! But they had not had milk for years. Not since the cow died.

She stole into the main room again, scraped a little sugar into a mug, and filled it with the steaming tea. Then she crept over to the settle bed.

Her grandmother was lying completely still. And before the girl had felt her hand, she knew that her grandmother was dead.

Her open eyes saw nothing. Her chin had fallen down, revealing the few small stumps of teeth in her gums. Her hands lay folded on top of the blanket, locked together like a knot in a rope. She was no more alive than the rocks along the shore, and she was just as immobile.

The girl was about to ask what she should do. But suddenly it dawned on her that this was exactly what she could not do, what she could never do again.

Then she sat down on the floor and burst into tears.

She cried for a long time. Her weeping was like a mighty wave that washed over her. Later it became a flowing stream, leaving her at last as warm and dry as a rock in the sun. Not a tear was left.

She realized that, just now, she did not need to ask her grandmother what she should do. She knew she should bury her. In the valley behind the crest of the hill. Beside Grandfather.

She found an old blanket and placed it on the floor next to the settle bed. Then she took hold of her grandmother and pulled her down onto the blanket. She tied the blanket together at the bottom and then grasped the opposite end and pulled. And so she started on the long journey, from the house, by the path along the brook, to the other side of the hill's crest, and up into the valley.

It took her all morning to reach her grandfather's grave. When she finally got there, she was so tired that her legs shook beneath her and everything reeled before her eyes. She sat down until her dizziness subsided. Then she walked back to the house to rest.

The first thing she saw when she came into the main room was that the fire had died down. She had completely forgotten about it. Quickly, she plucked a bit of wool out of her grandmother's big gray shawl, which was hanging on the back of the chair.

Then she grabbed a stick and poked around in the ashes until she finally found a single ember. Placing the tuft of wool over it, she blew carefully. The fire took hold of the fine hair and a flame leapt up. Without hesitating, she held a twig of heather out over the flame, and the fire ran farther up into the dry whisk. She piled on more heather, then small pieces of driftwood, and at last a large log. The flames caught hold of it, and the fire was saved.

She sat down on the floor and drank the cold, sweet tea that remained in the mug. She had to make do with the one mugful, for the tea she had let stand in the kettle had become so bitter that it was undrinkable.

Before leaving the house again, she fed the fire a piece of timber that was so large it would be able to burn for many hours. Then she walked back to the valley.

The valley opened up down toward the brook. Far away you could see the white house, bright against all the greenery. Behind it the sea shimmered in the sunlight and became one with the whitish blue sky.

The girl laid her grandmother a couple of meters from the heap of stones where her grandfather lay. She carefully covered her grandmother's body and face with the blanket before she began to gather stones and slabs of rock.

First, she made a square border of very large rocks around the body. Inside it she piled up all the stones she could find, until her grandmother was completely hidden. Then she stepped back a bit and compared her grandmother's grave with her grandfather's. She could see that the pile was not yet large enough if the two graves were to be the same. So even though sweat was dripping from her and her legs sometimes failed her, bringing her to her knees, she continued. Each time she had to go farther and farther away to find new stones.

At last she was satisfied. Long wisps of hair stuck to her cheeks, and both her knees were bleeding, but she no longer noticed. She sat down on a rock a short distance from the graves and looked out across the sea. The sun was just about to set.

A song! Now she was supposed to sing a song. Her grandmother had taught her that. But the only one she could recall was an old sea chanty:

From the sea have I come
and to the sea my way I wend.
I shall meet my one true love
and be parted from my friend.

She could not remember any more, so instead she began to sing something she herself made up:

My grandmother has passed away from me.
My grandmother is dead.
She was so sweet, so sweet to me,
but now she is dead.

The sun had disappeared, leaving the sky a grayish pink, which turned grayish blue if one looked at it long enough.

The girl could not think of anything more, so she began to sing about what she was seeing:

A crow is flying alone.
My grandmother is alone.
No, she is not alone,
for four sparrows are flying past,
and two crows are flying past.

Two crows never fly alone,
my grandmother is like a crow flying,
a crow that is off with its mate flying.
Two crows never fly alone,
and death is never, ever past.

Then she grew silent. For the last sentence she had sung had come all by itself. She did not understand it, and it frightened her.

The two crows disappeared as two black dots out over the sea, and she got up from the cold rock and walked home.

4

Several days later she saw the two crows again. They came flying from out over the sea, across the cove, and farther down along the shore.

It seemed as if they were calling to her. She stood still, listening to their hoarse screeches and watching them until they had disappeared. Then she turned around and walked back to the house.

It was clean and warm in the room. The floor was swept, and the flames were dancing in the hearth, but it was much too quiet. She missed the sounds of her grandmother in the settle bed, the coughs, the rustling with the blanket and pillows, her voice—especially when she said, "My chick."

The girl could hear that voice inside her all the time. It kept her going, got her to bank the fire with coals in the evening and to start it in the mornings. It got her to go out and gather mussels, to clean and sort them; indeed, it got her to eat them. She had the feeling that, without that voice, she would have just sat down and waited to die.

But now the two crows had interfered. "Come along, come along," they had screeched, showing her the way, and she could not stop thinking about them.

In the middle of the night she awoke with a start and did not know whether it was the memory of her grandmother's cough or the crows' screeching that had awakened her. It was completely dark in the room, and from one corner came a quiet scurrying.

Even though the girl knew that it was only the mouse, she called out into the darkness: "Grandmother, is it you?"

And the mouse answered by becoming quiet as a mouse.

———

The next day she did not start the fire. Instead she swept up the ashes from the hearth, carried them down to the beach, and scattered them along the water's edge. She went back to the house and lifted up the lid of the settle. There, she found a large kerchief, which she spread out on the floor. She placed her few pieces of clothing on it and tied it securely to her grandfather's old walking stick.

Then she arranged her grandmother's large gray woolen shawl over her black dress, swung the walking stick up on her shoulder, carefully locked the door behind her, and began to walk down along the shore.

After many days, during which she had stayed close to the water, living off raw mussels and sleeping on the ground, she reached a hamlet. A small group of houses stood on both sides of a narrow fjord, which cut its way inland. Farthest in, the fjord was no broader than a large stream, but it was deep, so people could sail their small dories all the way up, where they were protected from the sea.

The houses were whitewashed and resembled her

grandmother's, and they all stood with their broad sides turned out toward the narrow road that ran along the water.

The girl had never seen so many houses in one place, but there were not many people—two men in a boat at sea and a pair of toddlers who came running toward her from one of the houses. Shortly before reaching her, they stopped and stared, perplexed.

The door of the house was thrown open, and a housewife rushed out, grabbed one child with each hand, ran into the house again, and slammed the door behind her. The girl could hear the children crying and the woman scolding.

The door of another house opened, and another housewife came out and walked right up to her. She was older than the first, smaller and broader. Her hair was pulled back from her forehead and twisted into a tight knot on top of her head.

"Who in the world are you, and what are you doing here?" she asked, gazing intently.

The girl did not know how to answer.

"What's your name?" asked the woman impatiently.

"My grandmother called me her chick. But she's

dead now," the girl explained. She could not remember if there had ever been anyone who had called her anything else.

"*'Chick,'*" snapped the woman. "That's not a name, that's what something is."

She stood for a bit looking at the girl with the large gray shawl over her black dress, her dark hair gathered at her neck in a braid and her curved nose sticking out from her thin face.

"But you do resemble a crow, girl," she said.

"Yes," the girl hurried to say. "That's what I'm called. 'Crow-Girl.'"

"Peculiar name," mumbled the woman, scratching the corner of her mouth with one finger. "I hope you're not a bird of ill omen."

The girl shook her head.

"Are you a good worker?" the woman asked.

"Oh, yes," answered the girl. "I can light a fire and gather driftwood and mussels and sea kale and snails, and carry water, clean fish, and cook. I can feed a whole family," she said, and added in a low voice, "that is, if it isn't too big."

"Can you clean house, too?" the woman wanted to know.

"Yes," said the girl.

"Well then, I guess you had better come with me," said the woman, and started for the house.

The girl followed.

"Thanks . . . uh," she said.

"You can call me madam," said the woman over her shoulder.

"That's a funny name."

"Name," barked the woman. "That's no name; that's something you are. Come on, now!"

The main room was off a hallway just as at home. The room was bigger, but because there was a lot more furniture in it, it seemed smaller. Large chests and settles lined all the walls, and out in the middle of the stone floor stood a table with chairs around it.

What really distinguished it from the room in her grandmother's house was the pervasive aroma of food. A large black iron pot bubbled over the hearth, and the girl could feel her nostrils quivering as she approached it.

"Are you hungry?" asked the woman.

The girl nodded.

"Well, if it can't be otherwise, you had better have

something to eat. I usually don't believe in paying before the work is done."

The woman went over to the pot, lifted the lid, and ladled a large portion into a bowl. She took a wooden spoon from a drawer in the table and pointed at a chair with a wicker seat next to the fireplace.

"You'll sit there," she said.

The girl quickly sat down.

"Well, you could probably do with some flesh on your bones," said the woman. "Otherwise we'll surely not get much use of you." She handed the bowl to the girl.

Mutton boiled with potatoes until the meat was as tender as butter and the potatoes had completely dissolved and were infused with the taste of the meat. And afterward a cup of scalding hot tea with milk and sugar.

"You can start by sweeping," said the woman, taking the empty mug, "since you surely won't mind working for your food?"

"No, not at all," said the girl, and hurriedly grabbed the broom.

"First, put up the chairs," said the woman. "How

else will you manage to sweep where they're standing?"

The whole day the girl worked, scrubbed, fetched water, cleaned fishnets, and carried in wood from the shed behind the house. In the evening came her reward: a large bowl of soup boiled on the mutton bones, thick with chopped kale, root vegetables, and large oats, and a hunk of bread along with it.

The neighbor woman had stopped by.

"So, Crow-Girl, do you like the food?" she asked, and it sounded almost friendly.

The girl nodded.

"Who in the world is she?" the neighbor wanted to know. "I was quite frightened when I saw her standing out in the road. There's such a lot of riffraff passing by."

"It is surely half a year since we last had strangers in these parts," objected the woman. "But you are right, riffraff they were."

She took a gulp of tea and continued. "As for this one, she is only a poor orphaned thing. She lived with her old grandmother, who's now dead. Yes, it's a hard world. But now she can stay here, so she won't have to knock about on the roads any longer."

"You're a good person," said the neighbor, and got up. "I had better get over to the little ones again, before they do too much damage. Although I have tied them to the bed. Lucky are they who have such a big girl in the house. And since you don't have someone yourself, you'll surely get some use of her." She nodded in the direction of the Crow-Girl.

"That's not what it's all about," said the woman, offended. "I can manage by myself. But to earn one's daily bread has never hurt anybody."

"No, no, I certainly didn't mean it like that. I realize that you have taken her in because you are so good-hearted."

The woman ate up the words and nodded, satisfied, and they parted at the door as if they were good friends.

A short while later, her husband came home. He and a neighbor had been out fishing, and he brought back a bucket of cod, which the Crow-Girl was put to cleaning and salting so that they could later be dried on the rocks behind the house. Afterward, the woman accompanied the girl up the stairs to the attic, where a fishing net hung stretched out like a hammock. There lay a pillow and a blanket, and that was her bed.

Feeling full and tired, she clambered up, wound the shawl and blanket around herself, and fell asleep.

5

The next morning she awoke not knowing where she was. She sat up and the hammock began to swing from side to side. A dusty beam of sunlight from a peephole in the gable exposed a sheep's carcass dangling from a hook in the ceiling. Behind the hammock, over by the chimney, hung a couple of legs of lamb and some bundles of dried flatfish.

A voice called from below, and the Crow-Girl remembered at once where she was.

When she came down and opened the door to the main room, the woman was standing there wailing. "Just look at my shawl," she said. "It got caught on the firewood basket, and now a hole's been torn in it. I surely can't go anywhere with that."

The shawl was old, and the hole looked as if it was from wear.

"But perhaps I could borrow yours, just while I go visiting," said the woman.

"Yes, of course," said the Crow-Girl, and handed her the shawl.

"It's a very lovely shawl," said the woman. "Wherever did you get one like this? Surely you have gotten it honorably, for you are, of course, not also a magpie stealing everything it sees, are you?" And then she laughed as if she had said something funny.

"It was my grandmother's."

"Well, anyone could say that," and then the woman pinched the Crow-Girl's cheek and shook her slightly until she noticed her glance. "Well, well, little one, you can surely understand that I'm kidding."

The Crow-Girl nodded but did not think it was at all funny.

"Can you make mutton stew?" the woman asked.

"I can learn," said the Crow-Girl.

"There are potatoes out in the shed. Peel them.

And then carve a piece of meat from the sheep's carcass that's hanging in the attic, and cut that into pieces. Put it in the pot, alternating meat and potatoes and a bit of salt, then add a little water. And don't let the fire go out."

"I never have," said the Crow-Girl.

"Well, well," mumbled the woman, "there's always the first time. And no taking anything that doesn't belong to you."

The Crow-Girl started to prepare the food, peeling potatoes, cutting meat, filling the pot. She enjoyed being alone in that large room. Then she suddenly heard a deep cough from the other end of the house. She had left the door to the hall open to let in some fresh air; otherwise she would never have noticed the sound in that long house.

She slipped over to the room at the other end of the house and carefully opened the door a crack. A raw, rank odor met her. The hollow coughing was coming from a settle bed, where she could discern a figure.

"Well, come on in," said a man's voice.

The Crow-Girl moved closer.

"That's right, come over here!"

She stepped all the way over to the bed. An old man stretched out his hand and took hold of her arm with an iron grasp. She leapt back, terrified, but he held on so tight that she could not get away.

"Ha, ha," he brayed. "That scared you, I bet. You probably didn't think a weakling could be so strong, but it's my legs that are no good. There's nothing wrong with my arms, by Jove. And what are you sneaking around for? You won't find anything here, for the little there is I'm lying on. No, but you should see the other side of the house. That's where the chests are full."

"I know," said the Crow-Girl. "That's where I've just come from."

"I see, and what did you find there?"

"Nothing. I was just fixing the food."

He let go of her arm, and she rubbed it where he had held it.

"Food," he said. "What kind of food are you making?"

"Mutton stew."

"Do you have that often?"

"We had it yesterday, too."

The old man sat up in the bed with a start. "That stingy hag," he hissed. "She comes in here with a bowl of cold, thin soup and a piece of stale bread and says that that's all she has. But if I give her one of my gold coins, she'll get something better—as if she herself didn't have enough."

He struck his fist down on the chair next to the settle. "Never," he said fiercely, "never will she get them. It'll be over my dead body."

Coughing, he sank back against the pillows. "And she knows that, and that's why she treats me like dirt. She hopes I'll die from it, but she can just wait. She can just wait! Weeds are tough to kill, and it's happened before that a father has outlived his daughter." Then he cackled to himself.

While they were talking, the Crow-Girl began to feel chilled. It was as if the cold streamed out from the whitewashed walls and up from the stone floor. She clasped her arms about her, wishing she had her shawl. Then she saw that the hearth was empty, even of ashes. The old man must be cold through and through.

"Shouldn't I start a fire?" she suggested.

The man looked at her, confused, as if warmth was

something he had forgotten. So without waiting for an answer, she hurried into the other room to get some heather twigs and firewood and prepared a small heap of them. Then she fetched a burning branch and lit a fire for the man.

When she turned around and looked at the old man, she could see that his eyes were shining at the sight of the flames.

He said, "And if you could also get me a bowl of that mutton stew, then . . ." He dug in under the pillows and found a small silver coin, which he handed to her. "But don't show it to anyone. Promise me!"

The Crow-Girl nodded and went in to get a bowl of stew for him.

"And you'll come every day and start the fire?" he said when she handed the bowl to him.

"I promise," said the Crow-Girl, adding more wood to the fire before she left him.

She was alone in the main room the whole day. Not until the evening did the woman and her husband come back.

"What a lovely shawl this is," said the woman as

she took it off and draped it over a chair. "And now you shall see what I have for you in return."

She went over and pulled out a drawer in one of the chests and handed the girl a child's shawl, black with gray squares and a worn fringe.

"Thank you," said the Crow-Girl. "Is it for me?"

"The old one is, after all, too large for you, even if it is a good shawl. And since you were so kind as to give it to me, I thought I would give you the one I myself wore as a child."

"But . . ." the Crow-Girl began.

"What's more, if you can imagine, *my* grandmother made it for me when I was small."

"But . . ."

"Besides," said the woman, looking the Crow-Girl directly in the eyes, "I have not been chilly at all today as I usually am. And surely you don't want me to go around being chilly, do you, little Crow-Girl? For you are certainly not a bird of ill omen?"

"Of course not," said the Crow-Girl, frightened.

The woman pinched her cheek, shook her slightly, and said, "Well then, the matter is settled."

The Crow-Girl didn't know what to say.

"And now let us see whether you can make mutton stew," said the woman, sitting down at the table across from her husband. They waited while the Crow-Girl filled the bowls and served them.

When she had done so, she prepared a helping for the old man at the other end of the house. With the bowl of stew in one hand and a large piece of driftwood in the other, she was just about to go out the door when the woman stopped her.

"Where do you think you are going with that?"

"Over to your father."

"Do you intend to kill him? He cannot stand such rich food; it will ruin his stomach. Put that bowl down," the woman ordered.

The Crow-Girl put the bowl on the table, and the husband, who had already emptied his, started eating from it.

The woman went out into the hallway between the rooms, where there was a crock of kale soup from the day before. She half filled a bowl and splashed some water on top.

"You see, it mustn't be too warm or too thick," she said. "He can't tolerate that at all." She handed the bowl to the Crow-Girl along with a chunk of dry bread. "And the bread mustn't be fresh; it would be too sticky for his stomach," she explained. "And what do you think you are going to do with that piece of wood?"

"Put it on the fire."

"On the fire! Are you crazy, girl? There's scarcely enough firewood to cook the food. And you're thinking of making a fire for the old man. Just for his entertainment."

"I can gather driftwood tomorrow."

The woman tossed her head back, laughing.

"Gather, indeed, that's a good one. That's what everyone does, as soon as there's been the least bit of wind. How much wood do you think it takes to keep the pots boiling in all these houses?"

"I'll very likely find some," said the Crow-Girl. She turned her back and went off with not only soup and bread but firewood as well.

6

The Crow-Girl kept her word. The next day she got a piece of rope from the outbuilding and set off along the shore.

She knew that most people would rather stay indoors during a storm and would therefore not know how high and how far the water could reach. And she had noticed that the children who gathered firewood nearly always went all the way down to the water's edge. So the Crow-Girl began hunting farther inland, behind rocks and in hollows. And when she came to a stream, she walked up against the current and found driftwood along the banks where the sea had pushed its way in.

She gathered all that she could carry, tied the rope around it, and took it back to the house. Then she left again for a new load. She continued like that most of the day.

At last the woman came out into the yard. "How are you managing to find all that?" she exclaimed at the sight of the firewood. "I don't understand. But," she added, "it doesn't help us much just now. It will have to age so that the salt can be rained out."

"I think it already has," said the Crow-Girl. "When did you last have a storm that was so violent that the water beat in across the road in front of the house?"

"Well, it was probably over half a year ago," said the woman.

"So it's all right," said the girl, "for that's how high up and far in I've gone to gather it."

"You are a strange child," said the woman, and shook her head. "But now you had better get started on dinner. People have to work for their food, you know. It doesn't fix itself."

A couple of days later the Crow-Girl walked up along the shore, in the direction she had come from. She remembered that during the last part of the trip she had crossed a brook that ran through a broad strip of valley, and there she counted on finding a lot of driftwood.

Sure enough, the silver-gray wood lay shining everywhere on the grassy slopes. It surprised her that the other children had not noticed it. They must walk with their noses toward the water's edge all the time.

It did not take her very long to collect as much as she could carry. So she sat down beside the brook and listened to its murmuring and looked out across the sea.

A spattering of raindrops as fine as mist forced its way in from the sea. She shivered under the thin shawl. Then she saw the two crows. They were walking around pecking in the seaweed at the edge of the water, searching for food, just as she had been searching for firewood. Suddenly they flew up, as if something had frightened them. They spread their wings wide, feathers splayed out like fingers wearing black gloves. Screeching hoarsely, they fled right over her head.

She got up to watch them go and could see that they flew in a large arc that avoided the hamlet before they continued down the coast.

She picked up the firewood and hurried back to the house.

In the afternoon she went in to see the old man and placed more wood on his fire. His room was cozy now. The stone walls and floor had sucked up the warmth and held it all night long while the fire was covered by embers.

"It's a good thing that you've come to work at the house," said the old man.

The Crow-Girl did not answer. She stood for a bit, deliberating. Then she said, "I think that once in a while you ought to give your daughter a coin for taking care of you."

"Why should I do that?" he growled. "Isn't it a daughter's duty to see to her parents' old age?"

"No doubt it is," said the Crow-Girl, "but a person has no need of money when he's dead."

"Well, no," said the old man, "he probably doesn't." Then he grew silent.

The Crow-Girl hurriedly slipped out of the room in order to avoid having to listen if he should start complaining again. She had just reached the staircase in the hallway when she heard him yell.

"I'll never do it. The way she treats me. It'll be over my dead body!"

In the evening the woman was quite friendly toward the Crow-Girl, praised her for her work, and asked if she liked the food.

The Crow-Girl sat on the wicker chair by the fireplace. And even though she ate until her stomach felt like a stone, the food did not really satisfy her. And even though she was right by the fire, it did not really warm her.

"How down in the mouth you look sitting there," said the woman. "You aren't getting sick, are you?"

The Crow-Girl shook her head. "I'm just tired," she said.

"It's probably all that firewood you've been dragging here," said the woman in a kindly way. "Maybe you should go to bed early and get some rest."

The Crow-Girl nodded and rose to clear the table.

"No, just let that be. I'll take care of it," said the woman.

Her husband sent her an amazed look, but she did not bat an eye.

Up in the attic the Crow-Girl wrapped herself in the blanket and laid her head on the pillow. But she could not sleep. All the while she continued to picture the two crows as they had flown, screeching, right over her head. They passed over at least a hundred times before she finally fell asleep.

She awakened with a start from a heavy black sleep.

"Get away!" the crows had shrieked. "Get away!"

She lay in the darkness, listening. Then she suddenly heard voices from the room below. Carefully, she crawled out of the hammock and sneaked over to a crack where she could see the light seeping up.

"If we take her in as our own, everything she owns will be ours," she heard the woman say.

The Crow-Girl knelt and peeked down through the crack.

"What can she own?" said the man. He was sitting at the table with his head propped against one hand, while he twisted a tuft of his long red beard with the other.

"Well, now, there surely has to be something. The shawl was all right, wasn't it? And then, you know, there's also a house," said the woman, leaning toward him from the other side of the table. "And then there is, of course, all that driftwood."

"Driftwood?" said the man. "Why, everyone has the right to gather that."

"Yes, that's why there isn't enough," said the woman.

"Well, she brings in several bundles a day."

"But for how long? Until there is no more. And when will a storm come along again? Now listen to me."

She told him her plan. They would sail the Crow-Girl home to her grandmother's house and let her stay there a couple of days to gather up driftwood. And then they would fetch her again and sail her and the timber back. And then they would sell the timber.

"If she lived by herself as she says, no one else is gathering wood there, so we can have her do it several times a year."

"How wise you are, woman," said the man. "But how will you get her to stay?"

"Why shouldn't she stay?" said the wife. "We are good to her. She gets both bed and board. Besides, you see, she has no place else to go."

Shivering, the Crow-Girl pulled back from the crack. She had begun to itch all over from listening to their talk. They would *never* get her grandmother's house! They would *never* get the right to plunder the little cove! She had to get away.

She forced herself to lean down over the crack to look one last time to see where the woman had put the shawl. It lay over the chair she was sitting on. And the chair stood with its back toward the door.

The Crow-Girl pulled out her knife and cut a large piece of meat from one of the legs of lamb. She could just make it out in the dim light. Afterward she cut off one of the bundles of dried fish and packed everything in her black kerchief, tying it securely to the walking stick. She worked speedily and quietly.

Then the light downstairs was put out, and the attic became pitch-black. The Crow-Girl fumbled her way over to the hammock, crept up into it, and lay waiting for a long time, until she heard snoring.

She slipped out of the hammock again, folded the woman's shawl in the dark, and placed it on the floor beside her bed. And as payment for her food, she placed the little silver coin she had received on top. Picking up her walking stick, she stole down the stairs to the hallway.

She took a loaf of bread from the box in the hall and stuck it in her bundle. Then she stood outside the door to the main room and listened for a long time. At last she could distinguish between two sounds of snoring: the man's breathing, which was deep and steady, and the woman's, which was fast and slightly wheezy. The Crow-Girl opened the door slowly and carefully.

Warmth and the reek from cooking and the odor of their bodies rose up to meet her. She knew where everything was. But the woman had left a footstool standing right in the middle of the floor, and that was what she stumbled over.

The woman awoke and sat up in bed. "Wake up!"

she said to the man. "What was that? Do you think it was a thief?"

The Crow-Girl remained on the floor. She lay completely quiet. She could tell that the woman was listening out into the darkness, and she held her breath.

Irritated, the man grumbled and turned over. "It was probably a mouse," he muttered, and snored on.

But the Crow-Girl could feel that the woman was vigilant.

Then she suddenly let out a scream. "A mouse! It was a mouse. It ran right across me. I'm going to light a candle, and you must get up and catch it."

"No, I won't," said the man. "It's the middle of the night! Lie down now, so a person can get some sleep. I'll borrow the neighbor's cat tomorrow."

The woman lay down, but the fright must have kept her wide-awake. It was an eternity before the Crow-Girl again heard her short, hectic snoring mix with the man's noisy breathing.

She crawled on all fours over to the chair and slowly pulled the shawl down from the chair-back. Turning around, she traced a large arc around the footstool as she moved toward the door.

She listened for a long time, until she was certain that she heard them both. Then she stood up and carefully pulled the open door shut behind her, threw the shawl about her, put the walking stick with the bundle on her shoulder, and left the house.

7

A pale crescent moon could be seen behind the tattered clouds rushing across the sky.

The crows had flown in an arc far from the houses, so the Crow-Girl decided to go inland rather than follow the coast. She found the narrow rutted trail leading up from the head of the fjord and began walking along it as fast as she could.

Time after time she turned to see if anyone was following her, but the road was deserted and the hamlet slept. The moon moved in and out of the clouds, but her eyes quickly grew used to the dark, and the thought that she had to get away drove her on.

The narrow road met a broader road that went in the same direction as the coastline. She continued down the wide one, pausing only for short rests.

She walked the whole night and most of the next day, until she was so tired that her legs could hardly support her. So she left the road and climbed up behind some rocks, where she found a hollow she could rest in. She ate a bit of the lamb and drank water from a nearby brook.

Then she lay down and fell immediately into a dreamless sleep that lasted until the next morning.

When she awoke, she felt better than she had in a long time—as if someone had relieved her of a large load of firewood that she had borne on her shoulders without realizing it.

She got up, stretched, and looked around. Far away she glimpsed the sea, which calmly mirrored the blue of the sky. In the other direction, the gray-and-green land stretched out before her eyes, and there, farther down the road, another road turned off, leading to a couple of low gray buildings that were hunched beneath a pair of windblown trees.

Her first thought was to hurry past the place when

she came to it. Then she caught sight of the two crows. She could just make them out as two black spots among the gray trees, but the wind carried their screeches over to her.

She gathered up her things and started across the grass and stony ground, toward the house in the distance. She thought the crows screeched, "Here it is. Here it is."

She had to cross back and forth between the stone fences, which showed that the ground had once been cultivated. Fencing was meant to keep out sheep. Now ferns stood tall behind the low walls.

When she got close to the house, she stopped. It looked deserted: no smoke from the chimney, no people in the farmyard. The crows flew up from the trees and sat on the ridge of the roof. The Crow-Girl plucked up her courage and went over to the house.

The first person she met was a little boy who came to the doorway. He was not very tall; he scarcely reached up to her waist. His skin was brown and his hair was flaxen.

"What's your name?" she asked.

"Doup," said the boy.

"Doup," answered the Crow-Girl. "I've never heard that name before. I'm called Crow-Girl."

"Doup," said the boy, grabbing her hand and beginning to pull her.

The Crow-Girl laid her bundle down on the ground and let him lead her. He drew her into the house and over toward the hearth.

"Doup," he said again.

Above the cold ashes hung a pot.

"Doup," said the boy, pointing to the pot.

The Crow-Girl lifted the lid. At the bottom of the pot was some moldy soup.

"Doup," said the boy, satisfied, and let go of her hand.

"Soup!" exclaimed the Crow-Girl. "You want some soup. But, little one, you can't eat that. It's much too old. Now just look what I have for you."

She ran to retrieve her bundle, got out the bread, and gave him a large piece, but it was as if he did not understand that it could be eaten.

"Doup," he cried, and continued to point to the pot.

The Crow-Girl broke off a piece of the bread, hid it in her hand, and put her hand inside the pot. Then she brought her hand up again and gave him the bread.

"Soup-bread," she said. "There's nothing better."

The boy looked at her, amazed, and then began to cry.

She repeated the performance, and this time he accepted the bread and plopped it into his mouth. He pointed again to the pot and said, "Mush Doup."

And the Crow-Girl continued to break off pieces of bread, dipping them in the pot and handing them to him, until all the bread was eaten and the boy had had his fill.

Then she turned around to see what the room actually looked like—and stared right into a pair of eyes that were peering at her but seemed as if they were seeing nothing.

A man with his head supported in his hands was sitting behind the table by the wall opposite the fireplace. He must have been sitting there the whole time that she was feeding the boy. The Crow-Girl got up and walked over toward him.

"Hello," she said. "I am Crow-Girl. What is the boy's name?"

The man gave her a look filled with pain. His

light, gray-sprinkled hair was unkempt, and his beard-stubble was long. In the middle of that pale face his eyes shone like two blue lakes. He did not answer her.

"Where's the boy's mother?" asked the Crow-Girl.

The man continued to gaze at her with that empty look.

"Dead," he whispered, and suddenly rose and left the house.

Running over to the door, the boy stood looking after him.

"Pa, Pa," he called, but his father was already far out on the moor that bordered the house.

"Come here, little Doup!" called the Crow-Girl. "You can't catch him anyway. And I probably can't either. Let's see what you and I can do here instead."

She sat down on a chair and looked around. Doup came over to her and tried to crawl onto her lap. She took hold of him, pulling him the rest of the way up.

She could see that it had once been pleasant here. The room reminded her of her grandmother's, with not too much and not too little. But now it looked terrible: unmade settle beds, dirty clothes, dust and dirt and ashes on the floor, and something that looked as if it could have come from Doup's bottom.

She looked down at him, right into his dirty, tousled hair.

"You must have a bath, little Doup, really you must," she said, putting him down on the floor. "So we need to start a fire. I've been told how one does it, but I've never tried it."

First, she swept the hearth clear of ashes and prepared a pile of the driest heather twigs that she could find from the heap out in the hall.

Next, she drew out a piece of half-burned wood from beneath the ashes. With her knife she bored a small hole in it. Then she found a long stick and sat down close to the hearth. Holding the piece of wood in place with her feet, she put the stick in the hole and rolled it between her palms. She continued doing this for a very long time.

Doup watched with interest.

"Oooo," he exclaimed, when eventually a very slender column of smoke arose from the hole.

The Crow-Girl continued to roll the stick; next, she quickly held a tuft of wool over by the hole, but she did not succeed in lighting it. She had to try three times before the wool caught fire so she could move it over to the pile of twigs. At last they went up in flames.

The flames hungrily leapt up about the heather twigs and devoured them instantly. The Crow-Girl piled on several more and then added larger pieces of wood, until she and the boy felt the warmth radiate toward them and the fire lit up the room.

"Oh, oh, warm, warm," said Doup, holding his hands out toward the fire.

"Yes, it is warm. Be careful," said the Crow-Girl.

She poured water into a kettle and hung it over the fire. And in the evening, when the man returned, Doup had been scoured pink and clean amidst loud screams, the floor had been swept, and the room was fragrant from fried, smoked fish.

"This is for you," said the Crow-Girl, placing a plate of fried fish in front of the man.

He just sat there with his head in his hands and stared straight ahead without seeing anything at all.

Doup had hold of his fish with both hands and munched loudly and contentedly.

"Pish," he exclaimed with delight at each mouthful.

The Crow-Girl thought the man looked so terribly sad that she wanted to console him, but she did not know how. She cleared her throat, then said, "Is it long since Doup's . . . the boy's mother died?"

The man stared blindly out into space and did not answer her.

"Mine pish, mine," exulted Doup.

"How did she die?" asked the Crow-Girl.

Silence.

"My grandmother is dead, too, so now I am all alone," she continued. "We lived by a little cove, but I left. I walked along the coast and came to some houses by a fjord. There I lived with a woman and her husband, but I didn't want to stay with them, for they were only out to get my grandmother's place."

"Pish, pish," Doup called out across his empty plate.

She handed him another fish.

"I miss her so," she then said to the man.

"Just shut your ugly mouth!" he screamed, striking his fist on the table.

He got up and left the house once more, while the Crow-Girl and Doup silently finished eating. Afterward she and Doup fell asleep in one of the settle beds.

8

When she got up the next morning, the man was again sitting at the table with his chin in his hands, staring vacantly into space.

She crawled very carefully out of the settle bed in order not to awaken Doup or disturb his father.

She dug the coals out of the ashes and kindled the fire; then she walked over to the doorway and looked out across the landscape.

The sea fog had pushed its way in from the open water, and a thin drizzle wrapped the land in mist. All the colors were dampened into gray and brown, from the sky's mouse-gray to the heath's wet, black-brown pelt. The leaves of the trees hung withered and black, and water dripped from their tips. From the heather came a quiet calling, as if from a bird. Otherwise everything was still.

Then came a crash from within the room. The Crow-Girl rushed in and saw Doup's father holding a chair above his head, which an instant later he splintered to bits on the one he had already smashed.

Doup, completely stupefied, stood in the middle of the room while back slats and chair legs flew about his ears. The Crow-Girl ran over, grabbed him, and pulled him over to the doorway. The maddened man tipped the table until the plates and mugs fell to the floor and smashed to pieces, and the edge of the table hit the floor with a hollow crash.

He continued until nothing was left untouched. Settles were toppled, blankets torn, pillows turned into clouds of feathers. The kettle above the hearth was kicked down, and the fire disappeared in ashes, steam, and smoke.

When the man moved closer to where they were standing, Doup began to cry. The Crow-Girl picked up the boy and, carrying him, ran over to the outbuilding on the other side of the farmyard.

She stood there with him in her arms and became aware that they were both shaking all over. Doup's crying slowly diminished and little by little turned into long sniffs. He had his arms around her neck, and at last, exhausted, he laid his head down on her shoulder.

"There, there," said the Crow-Girl, patting him on the back.

Just then someone breathed on her neck. She became cold with fear and did not dare move. Something soft and warm touched her, and she let out a scream, leapt aside, turned around, and found herself looking into a pair of large eyes that belonged to a very small, very shaggy horse.

"Mine hoss, mine," shouted Doup, wanting to get down.

He said mine about everything he liked, the Crow-Girl had noticed. As soon as he was on the ground, he threw his arms around one of the horse's forelegs.

"Hey, watch out," said the Crow-Girl. "It could kick you."

"No kick, no kick," Doup assured her, while he shook his head to emphasize his words. "Mine, mine," he repeated.

In the meantime the sounds from the house had subsided. The Crow-Girl went out into the farmyard and stood for a moment, listening. Then she cautiously walked over to the doorway and looked in.

Everything was in chaos; it was as if a mighty storm had swept through the house. Even the windowpanes were broken. The damp odor from the dead fire hung in the air. And in the midst of that splintered world stood the man, drooping like a wounded animal.

The Crow-Girl walked very quietly over to him and looked into his blue, blue eyes. They were filled with tears, like lakes spilling over their shores after a long period of rain.

The Crow-Girl remained motionless beside him and didn't say a word.

"Take the boy with you when you go," he said. "Take the horse, too!"

The Crow-Girl nodded. The man turned on his heel and left the room. The last she saw of him was his stooped back as he made his way across the heath.

Out in the stable she found a sort of saddle with a wicker basket suspended on each side. She cinched the saddle on the horse. Doup could sit in one basket; she just had to find something to put in the other as a counterweight.

She went into the house and found her bundle behind an upended bench. The walking stick was broken, so she left it there. But she took the largest remnants of the blankets.

In a corner of the stable she found a sack of potatoes, which weighed about the same as Doup. With it and her bundle in one basket and Doup and the blankets in the other, she set out toward the road.

She would have resumed her journey down this road without giving it a second thought if the two crows had not come flying past.

"No, no, not that way! No, no, the other way!" she thought they screeched.

They themselves were flying in the opposite direction, up past the road leading to the houses by the fjord.

The Crow-Girl paused. She had no wish to come into the vicinity of that hamlet again.

"Cwo, cwo," called Doup, pointing at the crows. "Mine, mine."

So she followed them.

They had walked all of one day and most of the next when they reached the road down to the houses.

On the first day the sun had appeared, but now the rain had returned. In heavy showers it came driving in from the sea. The Crow-Girl had swaddled Doup in her shawl, and the tightly woven wool kept out every drop. He sat in the basket, warm and safe, talking to the horse, the Crow-Girl, and himself. From time to time, he fell asleep, so that his head with its flaxen hair jounced back and forth in rhythm with the horse's movements.

The Crow-Girl had wrapped a blanket around herself until only her face was uncovered. She kept warm by walking beside the horse while she held the reins.

The cloud cover was heavy, and twilight came early. It was nearly dark when the Crow-Girl heard a wagon come rumbling behind them. She pulled over to the side of the road so the wagon could pass.

The people driving by were talking loudly, and suddenly the Crow-Girl recognized the woman's voice. She hurriedly pulled the blanket up about her head.

"Don't worry," she heard the woman say. "We'll find her all right, that little thief. What does she think she's doing? To pay me with money she has stolen from my father!"

"Well, what if he really did give it to her?" the man said.

"Nonsense. As stingy as he is," snarled the woman. "He says that only to needle me."

The wagon rushed past, as the man shouted, "Get out of the way!" and let his whip snap across the back of the small horse.

"Rabble," exclaimed the woman. "The roads are teeming with scavenging riffraff."

Farther on, the wagon turned down the road toward the houses, and the Crow-Girl breathed a sigh of relief.

While the wagon was driving past, there had been a pause in the rain; now it started up again. She checked on Doup in his basket. He had rolled himself up at the bottom and lay beneath the shawl, sleeping with a thumb in his mouth. She felt his hand. It was quite warm. Then she put a piece of blanket over the basket. He could lie there keeping dry until she found a place where they could spend the night.

As she walked along, she could feel the water seeping through the blanket around her shoulders and neck. A single cold drop trickled down her back. Before long she would be thoroughly soaked, and it would be too dark to see anything at all.

Then, far ahead, she saw a campfire flickering in the darkness. Without thinking, she headed straight toward it.

But when she got closer, she stopped. Two dark figures were casting enormous shadows on the rock walls behind them. The figures sat stock-still, but the flames made the shadows dance.

"Who's there?" came an anxious voice from over by the fire.

"It's only me," called the Crow-Girl.

"It sounds like a child," the speaker said to the other person.

"Are you alone?" came the voice again.

"No, I'm with Doup."

"Who's Doup?"

"A little boy."

"And who are you?"

"Crow-Girl."

"Come on over then."

Now the Crow-Girl could hear that it was a woman who had made her voice as deep as a man's. She approached her.

"I won't cause any trouble," she hurried to say when she saw the knife in the woman's hand.

"No, of course not," said the woman, sticking the knife back in her belt. "Come get warm!"

There, at the base of the cliff, they were completely sheltered from the rain. The speaker was a grown woman, not quite young, but not old either. She looked tired and worn. Next to her sat a girl who appeared to be a couple of years younger than the Crow-Girl, but her face was hidden because she had pulled her kerchief so far forward.

"Welcome," said the woman. "Just pull the horse in here, too. There's enough room for all of us."

Doup was awake. He had pushed the blanket away and was sitting up in the basket. He looked around, confused. The Crow-Girl led the horse over close to the cliff, tied it, and lifted Doup down from the basket.

"What a little fellow you're traveling with," said the woman in a friendly way.

The Crow-Girl nodded. She sat down with him on the ground in front of the fire. He was warm and dry; she was thoroughly soaked and ice-cold. She stretched her hands out to warm them.

"Warm, warm," exclaimed Doup, blowing on his fingers.

"The weather has taken a terrible turn," said the woman. "We were lucky to find this place."

Then, suddenly, there was the sound of quiet sniffling. It was the girl. Her mother put her arm around her.

"I'm so hungry," said the girl.

"Yes, I know," said her mother, "but there's nothing we can do about it now. In a while you'll be asleep, and then you won't feel it."

"Yes, I will," whimpered the girl. "It wakes me up all the time."

"Wait . . ." said the Crow-Girl, and got up.

She had been so cold and wet that she had forgotten all about food. Now she fetched several potatoes and put them in the embers. Then she took the last of the smoked lamb and divided it between them.

"Thank you so much," said the woman. "We haven't had anything to eat for several days."

They each ate a small piece of meat in silence.

Then the woman said, "My name is Foula, and this is my daughter, Eidi. So you are Crow-Girl, and this is your little brother, Doup?"

"No, he isn't my brother."

While the potatoes lay roasting in the coals, the Crow-Girl told them her story. When she had finished, Foula said quietly, "Dear child. It sounds like it hasn't been easy."

Her voice was soft and the Crow-Girl burst into tears. Great sobs rose up in her like bubbles and made her shoulders shake with weeping. Foula gently stretched out her hand and caressed her cheek. The Crow-Girl laid her head down on Foula's lap and cried and cried while the woman stroked her hair.

Doup became frightened, but Eidi took him up on her lap and sat singing to him. Then he calmed down.

The Crow-Girl's weeping slowly quieted, and she straightened up again. A little later she raked the potatoes out of the fire and divided them. She did not take any herself. She felt her hunger was sated.

9

The next morning, when the Crow-Girl saw Eidi's face in daylight, she cried out in shock.

One eyebrow was torn, and under the bloody flap the girl's skin was black and blue and so swollen that there was only a narrow slit left for her to see through. But on the other side of her nose a curious light-brown eye was open and looking at her.

"What happened?" asked the Crow-Girl.

"It was my stepfather," answered Eidi. "He was going to hit my mother, and I wouldn't let him, so he hit me, too. Now we've left him." She raised her hand up to the wound. "Does it look terrible?" She looked quizzically at the Crow-Girl. The eye that could be seen looked sorrowful.

The Crow-Girl quickly shook her head.

"It'll look fine again," she said. "But why did he hit the two of you?"

Eidi shrugged. At that moment Foula came back from the brook, where she had washed. She had Doup in her arms.

"He's certainly not very fond of water," she said, setting him down.

He ran over to the Crow-Girl and put his arms around her neck.

"Oh my, oh my," he said. "Wet, oh my."

"I guess he's not been washed very often lately," said the Crow-Girl, pulling him up on her lap. "Isn't that so, you little scamp?"

"Oh my," said Doup, clinging to her. "Wet, ow, ow."

The Crow-Girl laughed.

"Come," Foula said to Eidi. "We had better get that eye bathed."

Together, they headed toward the stream. The Crow-Girl sat there, watching them go. She noticed that Foula limped.

Behind them the clouds were tinted by the sun. The rain had passed by in the course of the night, and here and there the blue sky peeked out between white, pink, yellow, and gray clouds. The grass and heather were dripping with water, and the air was cold and clear.

The Crow-Girl breathed deeply, leaned her head back, and gazed up at the enormous dome arching above her head.

"Look," she said to Doup. "We are sitting right in the midst of everything."

And Doup answered her with a long, unintelligible sentence that ended with a jubilant, "Wook!"

For breakfast each of them ate a cold potato from the night before.

"It was kind of you to share your food with us," Foula said to the Crow-Girl. "It's difficult to get it yourself when you are used to a man who both fishes and hunts. And when that failed, we always had a patch of land for growing potatoes and other vegetables. We also had a small flock of sheep."

She was quiet for a minute, then turned to Eidi. "So I have wondered whether he might not regret what he has done? Whether he might not have been so shocked that he would not do it again?"

"Oh, Mother, no!" exclaimed Eidi, hiding her face in her hands. "He promises that every time; then when he has been drinking, he forgets it again."

"Yes," said Foula, "but if we continue like this, we will die of hunger."

The Crow-Girl sat very quietly, not knowing what to say. Even Doup kept still and just played with the fringes on her shawl.

Suddenly there was a hoarse screech above her head, and she looked up. The two crows flew right over her and continued up along the road. She turned to watch them. When they were nearly all the way out on the horizon, she thought they swung off toward the coast, but they were so far away that she was not certain whether she could really see them.

A single screech! Right above her head. She let the memory of the sound sink into her, so that it vibrated within her like a chord, and she understood at once what the screech meant. It meant "Home."

"You can come along to my house," said the Crow-Girl.

Eidi raised her head, and joy spread from her light-brown eye out across her whole face.

"Oh, Mother, yes!" she cried.

Foula had looked at the Crow-Girl with a glimmer of hope in her glance. Then her face became shuttered and quiet again.

"There's enough room," said the Crow-Girl. "You two can have the larder. We can use the loft for storage."

"But what will we live on?" asked Foula doubtfully.

The Crow-Girl could see that she was already about to give up again. But the Crow-Girl did not lose hope so easily.

"Potatoes!" she suggested. "Didn't you say you had grown potatoes? There are still some left in the sack. And there is also a field. But it does have to be cleared," she added in a slightly lower voice.

Then she got up, walked over to the horse, retrieved the sack, and carried it over to Foula.

"There aren't very many," said Foula when she had looked in it. "But they can of course be divided. As long as there's an eye on each piece, it can become a plant."

"Oh, can't we do it?" begged Eidi. "I don't want to go back again."

"But what shall we live on while we grow them?" continued Foula. "No, Eidi, it won't work. We will have to go back. But I promise you that he will never hit you again." This time it was Foula's voice that sounded pleading.

But Eidi shook her head. "You know very well that you can't," she said. "And I would rather go hungry than be beaten. I'm going with Crow-Girl."

"We can gather mussels until the potatoes come," said the Crow-Girl. "And sea kale. There was enough food for my grandmother and me . . . Almost," she added, remembering the evenings she had gone to bed hungry.

"Well, all right then," said Foula finally.

The other three remained quiet as mice, waiting for what was to come.

"So let us go with Crow-Girl. But how we will manage, I just can't imagine," she added, looking at the three children.

They decided to continue following the road in order to make better time. Later they would head out to the sea and follow the coastline until they came to the cove. The Crow-Girl actually did not know of any other way back, and she did not know how many days she had spent walking from her grandmother's house to the hamlet by the fjord.

Eidi was so happy that they were going along that she walked beside Doup's basket and sang at the top of her lungs. Doup was delighted. The Crow-Girl led the horse, and Foula limped beside her, carrying a metal pail in her hand. In it she had the coals from the campfire. Its handle was made of wood, so she would not burn herself, and there were small holes in the sides so that the coals would not be choked.

The Crow-Girl wanted to start running. "Home, home" was singing within her. Home to the brook with the flat rock, sea, and sky, and the white house, the hearth, and . . . She stopped herself, for there was no grandmother to come home to.

Her steps slowed, and now she could feel that they had already traveled far. "Shouldn't we sit for a bit?" she suggested, and then realized that both Eidi and Foula had needed to do so for a long time.

They sat down a short way from the road and took turns warming their hands at the metal pail. Foula took the shoe and stocking off her bad foot and looked at her swollen ankle.

Doup went scouting behind some rocks and was only away a short time before he suddenly came rushing back to the Crow-Girl. "Mine Cwo," he shouted.

That was his way of saying Crow-Girl.

He grabbed hold of her clothing and tried to crawl up. On his heels came a black wire-haired dog, wagging its tail and looking as if it wanted to play with him. It was clear that Doup was terribly afraid of it, and the Crow-Girl hurriedly lifted him up so the dog could not reach him. He threw his arms around her neck and clung there tightly.

Following the dog, a man emerged from behind the rocks. He stopped and looked in amazement at the little party. Then he saw Doup and the dog.

"Glennie, come here!" he called, and the dog ran over to him and sat down.

"You have to forgive her frightening the young fellow," he said. "She's never done any harm to anyone. But how could such a little boy know that." He patted the dog on the head. "You can put him down now," he said to the Crow-Girl. "She'll stay here."

The Crow-Girl sat down with Doup on her lap.

"Sit down yourself," suggested Foula, handing the pail of coals up to him. "Here's something to warm your fingers on."

He took it, seated himself, and placed his hands around it. The Crow-Girl looked at him with curiosity. He wore a knitted cap on the top of his well-kept gray hair, which was cut off just above his shoulders. His cheeks were covered by a short gray beard that came to a point on his chin.

"Hey, that doesn't look any too good," he said suddenly, pointing to Foula's foot. "I hope you're not walking very far on it?"

"Yes, unfortunately," said Foula, sighing, "for the horse is too small to carry me."

The man shook his head.

"This will never do," he said. "All of you had better come home with me until that foot has gotten better. I don't live very far from here. Over there." And he pointed in the same direction that the crows had flown, in the direction of the cove.

10

The man's name was Rossan, and his house was quite small, with only one chimney, a single room downstairs, and an attic upstairs. But there was a fire on the hearth, food in a pot, a table with two benches, and a bowl, spoon, and mug for each of them.

The Crow-Girl could not remember anything ever before having tasted so good to her as the potatoes and meat and that strong tea with milk and sugar.

Not a word was spoken for a long time because they were all so busy eating. Even Doup, who was sitting on a pillow beside her, had grown silent from all the food he had stuffed into his mouth. He could scarcely close his jaws and had to spit half of it into the bowl again in order to chew the rest.

Suddenly the Crow-Girl heard sniffling and, looking up, became aware that right across from her Foula had broken into tears.

"Pay no attention," said Foula, smiling at her. "It's just because I'm so relieved that we are sitting here." She dried her tears with the back of her hand.

"Well, it must not have been pleasant to walk on that foot," said Rossan kindly.

And Foula's tears began to flow again. Then she had to laugh.

"As if there isn't enough to cry over," she said, "and here I sit weeping over a serving of mutton stew."

The others laughed with her.

"Would you like more tea to cry into?" Rossan asked Foula, and lifted the kettle. Eidi laughed until her eyes also welled up.

"Hey, are you starting now, too? Just watch out that your tea doesn't get cold, or is that perhaps your intention?" joked Rossan.

The Crow-Girl thought it was wonderful to laugh. It had been a long time since she had done so.

Doup looked at them with wide eyes. Then his face broke into a gigantic smile, and meat and potatoes rolled from his mouth down into his bowl again.

Rossan, who was sitting on a chair at the end of the table, leaned back with his arms behind his head. "What a cheerful party. Don't you agree, Glennie?" he said to the dog, who was lying before the hearth with a bone.

The dog wagged her tail so that it pounded the floor, and she continued gnawing.

Even though the house was small, there was room for all of them. The little horse was out in the stable munching oats beside Rossan's only cow. Foula was to sleep in the settle bed, where Rossan usually slept, and on the floor he made up a large bed of heather branches and sheepskins for the children.

"Where are you going to sleep?" asked the Crow-Girl.

"Come and take a look," he said, and started climbing up the steep stairs at the end of the room.

There was a window in the gable above the stairs, so when they reached the top, the Crow-Girl could see where the strange odor streaming toward them was coming from. Large bales of wool lay stacked along the sides of the room. White wool and gray wool, black and dark brown and tan—there were all the colors that wool can have. The Crow-Girl had never in her life seen so much wool at one time.

"I'll lie down over here by the chimney," said Rossan. "It's nice and cozy."

Glennie stood at the bottom of the stairs, whining and scratching the steps with her paws. She did not dare follow them.

"Is Glennie a real sheepdog?" asked the Crow-Girl.

"No," said Rossan, "she's just good at tending sheep."

Then they clambered down again, and Glennie wagged her whole body as though she had not seen Rossan for weeks.

The next day, when he went out to the sheep, Rossan took the Crow-Girl along. Eidi preferred to stay inside the warm house, and Doup and Foula could not walk so far.

It was a clear, cool morning. The sun had risen behind a thin mist of clouds, which lay like white veils pulled across the sky. A brook sought its way down toward the sea, which could be seen as a shining ribbon far out on the horizon. The Crow-Girl bent down, cupped her hands, and took a sip. The water was so cold that it chilled her teeth.

When they had reached the other side of the hollow in the valley, they saw the flock. The small, long-legged animals were scattered out across the countryside.

"They're doing fine here," said Rossan, looking satisfied.

"How so?" the Crow-Girl wanted to know.

"Well, you see, there are no bogs here. They are the worst. If a sheep falls in something like that, it can't be saved. The mire sucks it down, and if you try to get it out, you risk plunging in, too. So I check on them several times a day to see where they are going. There's no reason to disturb them here."

And they turned around and went back.

Inside it was snug and warm. A pot bubbled above the fire. The bed was made; Eidi and Doup sat on it

see where the strange odor streaming toward them was coming from. Large bales of wool lay stacked along the sides of the room. White wool and gray wool, black and dark brown and tan—there were all the colors that wool can have. The Crow-Girl had never in her life seen so much wool at one time.

"I'll lie down over here by the chimney," said Rossan. "It's nice and cozy."

Glennie stood at the bottom of the stairs, whining and scratching the steps with her paws. She did not dare follow them.

"Is Glennie a real sheepdog?" asked the Crow-Girl.

"No," said Rossan, "she's just good at tending sheep."

Then they clambered down again, and Glennie wagged her whole body as though she had not seen Rossan for weeks.

The next day, when he went out to the sheep, Rossan took the Crow-Girl along. Eidi preferred to stay inside the warm house, and Doup and Foula could not walk so far.

It was a clear, cool morning. The sun had risen behind a thin mist of clouds, which lay like white veils pulled across the sky. A brook sought its way down toward the sea, which could be seen as a shining ribbon far out on the horizon. The Crow-Girl bent down, cupped her hands, and took a sip. The water was so cold that it chilled her teeth.

When they had reached the other side of the hollow in the valley, they saw the flock. The small, long-legged animals were scattered out across the countryside.

"They're doing fine here," said Rossan, looking satisfied.

"How so?" the Crow-Girl wanted to know.

"Well, you see, there are no bogs here. They are the worst. If a sheep falls in something like that, it can't be saved. The mire sucks it down, and if you try to get it out, you risk plunging in, too. So I check on them several times a day to see where they are going. There's no reason to disturb them here."

And they turned around and went back.

Inside it was snug and warm. A pot bubbled above the fire. The bed was made; Eidi and Doup sat on it playing with the porridge spoons. And Foula was at the table, knitting a stocking.

"Well, I took the liberty," she said to Rossan, and lifted the knitting up so he could see it. "I need to use my hands, since, as you know, I'm in a fix with my feet."

"Feel free to go on knitting socks for me if you really want to. But if not, there's plenty of other handiwork here. There's so much wool lying in the attic that there's enough to keep us busy the rest of the winter. Knit I can do, but spin I can't. And yarn, after all, pays better than wool."

"We can do it," said Foula happily. "I see that you have a spinning wheel."

"Yes," said Rossan. "My sister used to come to give me a hand with it, but now she is too old to travel so far to prepare the little amount of yarn I need."

He sat for a moment, considering, while he scratched Glennie behind one ear. Then he said to Foula, "I have a proposition for all of you. If you will spin for me just half of the wool lying in the attic, each of you may choose a sheep from the flock when you leave. And their lambs go along." He looked from one to the other.

Foula nodded. "I think that sounds like a good agreement," she said. "Then we'll also have something to live on when we get to Crow-Girl's cove."

Eidi nodded, too, but the Crow-Girl was crestfallen.

"What do you say?" Rossan asked her.

"I can't spin."

And she knew that she did not much want to learn either, for it would mean that she would have to sit inside the whole day.

"So would you perhaps rather leave?"

The Crow-Girl shook her head.

"No, I would like to have a sheep, too," she said.

"Why, then, you can herd them."

The Crow-Girl looked at him. A smile spread across her face. Then it disappeared. "I don't know how to go about doing that either."

"I can teach you," said Rossan. "Glennie and I. And afterward I'll have time to repair the stable roof and all the other things that I never get done."

That was how the Crow-Girl became a shepherd. Each morning she set out to search for the flock. When the weather was good, she brought Doup along in the basket on the shaggy horse's back. He wouldn't leave the basket because he was afraid of the sheep when he was on the ground. When it poured rain, she went with Glennie alone.

She helped the sheep get free when they were caught in the thorny brush. Together with Glennie she drove them away from the treacherous bogs and up to the crests of the hills. She got to know each sheep and scratched it on the chest whenever it allowed her to. She called Glennie to her and shouted commands to her to run straight ahead, to the right, or to the left.

And sometimes she just shouted right up at the sky, because she was finally happy again to be alive.

11

One rainy afternoon a sorrowful bleating could be heard from the stretch of heath where the sheep were pasturing. The Crow-Girl followed the sound and came to the edge of a bog.

There was no water to betray it, only the feeling of a wet sucking that grew more apparent as one walked on the moss between the small, leafless bushes. The Crow-Girl was just about to turn back when she noticed a flat rock that stretched out a way into the bog. She crawled up on it and looked around.

And there, at the end of the rock, was the sheep she wanted most of all. Water had pooled around it, and its legs had already disappeared into the mire. The animal had no fight left in it and was now just looking up at her, bleating in despair.

The Crow-Girl lay down on her stomach on the rock and stretched her hands out toward the sheep. She could nearly reach it; she could feel its warm breath. But there was nothing to take hold of, no way to pull it up. And in her heart of hearts she knew very well that even if she had gotten hold of it, she would not have had the strength to free it. No one could free it. That which the bog had gotten hold of it would not give up again.

She sat up. The sheep's body had nearly disappeared. It was such a pretty sheep, dark brown with a still darker head and legs. She had scratched it on the neck and chest many times, and she knew that its wool was of the finest and softest sort.

"Oh no, little sheep," she lamented.

Now that dark head, raised high on its neck, was the only part of the sheep that could be seen. Its pupils were narrow and sharp, as if they had been cut with a knife. Its yellow eyes were staring blindly to every side, as the sheep bleated one last time before it disappeared into the bottomless swamp.

"Oh no," lamented the Crow-Girl again.

She had placed her hands over her face and sat rocking back and forth in an attempt to withstand the pain. All the time she saw before her the sheep's last, wild look. And each time she moaned at the sight.

"Oh no."

Glennie, though ordered to wait beyond the bog, had cautiously made her way out to the girl.

Now the dog sat down beside her and whined softly. But the Crow-Girl did not hear it. Glennie pressed her nose in under the girl's arm, but she just continued sitting and rocking with her hands before her face. Then the dog put her head back and howled like a wolf up at the rain-heavy clouds.

It was Rossan who found them. When it had begun to turn dark and they had not returned, he went out to search for them. It was Glennie's howling that had led him to them.

He got hold of the Crow-Girl and lifted her up to

take her home. She was so wet that water was pouring off her, and the front of Rossan's body became soaked from his holding her.

"It drowned, my sheep drowned," she sobbed.

"There, there," said Rossan. "That can happen. It happens to all shepherds. It's happened to me as well."

"My sheep," cried the Crow-Girl.

"There, there. We'll find another one for you. There are lots of sheep."

But it was as if his words did not get through to the Crow-Girl—as if she had enclosed herself in a shell where he could not reach her or console her.

And before long he did not even have the breath to talk but had to use all his strength to carry her home.

Back at the house Foula undressed her, rubbed her dry and warm, and put her to bed.

"Now she should just have a good night's sleep," she said, and tucked the sheepskins carefully around her.

The Crow-Girl's teeth were chattering. Eidi sat down beside her and held her hand. At first it was icy cold, but it soon became burning hot. The Crow-Girl was running a fever.

Eidi called her mother, and Foula came over to feel the Crow-Girl's forehead.

"She's very warm," she said, removing the skins and covering her with a thin blanket. "Get a mug of water," she said to Eidi.

But the Crow-Girl could not be persuaded to drink. It was as if she neither saw nor heard anything, as if she were somewhere else entirely.

"Eidi," said Foula, "sleep in the settle with Doup tonight. I'll stay here."

"Is she very sick?" asked Eidi.

Foula shrugged her shoulders, but Eidi could see how worried her mother was. And in the middle of the night when Eidi awoke, because Doup had happened to kick her, she saw that Foula was sitting on the bed with the Crow-Girl's head in her lap and that Rossan was sitting on a chair at the end of the table, knitting his stocking and watching over them. Then she fell asleep again.

The next day Foula and Rossan took turns getting some sleep, and at night they both kept vigil again.

Foula spent a lot of time trying to get the Crow-Girl to drink. Then she came up with the idea of pouring water in a bottle, tying a piece of leather over the opening, and poking a hole in it. She stuck the bottle in the Crow-Girl's mouth, and the water trickled slowly out so the girl could swallow it in small amounts.

But Eidi noticed that even if Foula was happy to have gotten the Crow-Girl to drink, she still had, right above the bridge of her nose, those two vertical lines that showed how anxious she was.

The Crow-Girl still hadn't spoken. She only moaned weakly once in a while.

She let out a groan each time a sheep drowned before her mind's eye. Black-and-brown, gray-and-white sheep were slowly swallowed up by a spongy, yellowish brown bog. At first there were just as many sheep as in Rossan's flock, then double that number; then double again—as if all the sheep in the whole world were destined to drown right before her eyes. And she felt her body as a great aching that was perpetuated by the death of each sheep.

After a while the sheep became smaller and

smaller, and finally little lambs were drowning, as, beside themselves with terror, they called to the mothers from whom they had strayed.

"No!" she screamed, and she thought she sounded like a crow screeching out across the winter-wet heath.

Then she felt that she had taken off and had begun flying away from the bog, out across the sea. She had a dizzying fear of falling and knew that if she gave in to it she would be doomed. So she kept herself afloat and discovered that the sea was not just beneath her but also above her and on all sides, as if she were contained within it.

And within the sea, in that void with water on all sides, a well-known voice said, "My chick, I am right here."

The void itself seemed to speak, and the voice was her grandmother's.

"Oh, Grandmother," called the Crow-Girl, "let me die. Won't you, please? I can't stand it anymore."

"My chick," came the voice again, and this time the sound of it gently stroked her brow, and the touch calmed her. "You are far too young to die. Come, I'll take you back now."

And it was as if a pair of great, gentle hands carried her and carefully laid her on the bed, with her head on Foula's lap.

A cool hand stroked her forehead, and a voice softly hummed a slow melody, which wafted through the air like a thread of the finest silky-soft wool.

12

Slowly the Crow-Girl got better. She lay in bed while Foula spun and Eidi carded. The sound of the spinning wheel and the combing cards and the crackling fire consoled her, and Doup's persistent attempts to pull her up from bed even made her smile.

"Mine Cwo," he coaxed, "come see little puppy."

"I can see her quite well from here," she said, and looked over at Glennie's black head sticking up from the dog's basket.

Then it dawned on her that there was something not quite right about it. "Hey," she said, "why is Glennie here when Rossan is out with the sheep?"

Foula smiled as she continued to spin. "Doup is right. Glennie had two pups while you were sick."

"May I see them?" begged the Crow-Girl.

"If she'll let me," said Foula, and went over to the basket.

Glennie whined uneasily when Foula picked up one of the pups, but she let her do it.

Foula carried the tiny pup over to the Crow-Girl, who took it and held it for a moment in her hands. The creature was no larger than her palm. Then Foula carried it back again.

The Crow-Girl looked longingly after it.

"Would you like us to put the basket over by your bed?" asked Foula.

The Crow-Girl nodded.

And so Eidi and Foula carried the basket over to the bed, while Glennie followed, whining.

Each morning when the Crow-Girl awoke, the first thing she did was to look down into the basket at Glennie and the pups.

She would sit in bed for long periods of time holding Doup on her lap, talking about and watching the two "little puppy," as he called them. But even though she seemed happier, she was still so tired that she had to join Doup in taking an afternoon nap.

Eidi and Foula worked diligently, and bundles of brown, white, gray, and black yarn piled up in a basket in the corner.

One day, Rossan announced that he would go to the market in the nearest town and sell what had already been spun—if Eidi would look after the sheep a couple of times a day. She was happy to do so. Then he asked the Crow-Girl if he might borrow the horse so he could transport all the yarn. She said yes on Doup's behalf, for she considered the horse to be his.

Rossan set off, and Foula and Eidi continued spinning and carding. The Crow-Girl lay watching them.

Illness had left its mark on her face. Her eyes were deeply sunken in their sockets, and her cheekbones prominent beneath her pale skin. Her nose stuck out below her dull hair like a curved beak. Only her eyes shone; large and dark blue, they looked at the world as if they were discovering it for the first time.

The sun came in through the windows, dividing the room into strips of light and shadow. Eidi sat in a band of light holding one of the combing cards on her thigh and the other in her hand, and between those two cards she worked the wool into the long, narrow wisps that Foula spun the yarn from.

The only hint in Eidi's face of the blows she had received from her stepfather was a white scar in one light-brown eyebrow. Her thin, bruised face was now round and smooth, and her hair hung down her back in a red-gold braid that ended in a large curl right above her waist. Foula had combined light-brown and dark-brown yarn in the braid, and Eidi had found a red-brown feather and stuck it in at the bottom.

Foula sat in the shadow between the two windows. She no longer limped, and the sad, tired expression had left her face. She seemed quite calm and satisfied as she sat by the spinning wheel—as though she was sitting someplace she wanted to be.

Her hair was a little lighter and a little less golden than Eidi's, owing to its scattering of gray. But it was still thick, and it curled up in locks that had fallen down from the heavy bun atop her head.

The Crow-Girl looked down at herself and sighed.

"What is it?" asked Foula gently, without raising her eyes from her work.

"It's my hair," said the Crow-Girl.

Foula looked over at her. Her dark hair was tangled and bristled out on all sides.

"Shall I braid it for you?"

The Crow-Girl nodded.

Foula sat down on the bed and brushed the girl's hair, dividing it into two braids and tying the ends with white bows made of yarn. When she was done, the girl's hair was just as dark and smooth as it had been before she took ill.

Foula went back to the spinning wheel, and the Crow-Girl laid her head down on the pillow and closed her eyes.

At first, everything was black behind her eyelids. Then some small shining dots came dancing out of the dark, and suddenly an image clearly appeared to her of the little white house by the cove. She felt a tug of longing for it and the sea, for the grass and the brook. Then the picture disappeared once more, and darkness returned.

She awoke to the sound of Foula's voice.

"I wonder whether we shouldn't ask Rossan if we might stay here," she said to Eidi.

The Crow-Girl felt her breast aching at the words, and she happened to cough. Eidi looked over at her, frightened.

The Crow-Girl turned onto her side with her back to them. She felt that she had to get back to the cove whether Foula and Eidi came along or not, but the thought of doing it alone with Doup made her desperate.

"Oh, but no, Mother," said Eidi. "Why should we do that? We promised Crow-Girl we'd go with her."

"Yes, but we are doing well here, and we can be of some use. Rossan, after all, needs somebody who can help him with the wool, and Crow-Girl can help him with the sheep. And look at Doup; see how much he has grown since we came here. His cheeks are round now. Can you remember how little and thin he was when we first saw him? With snot running out of his nose all the time?"

The Crow-Girl knew that she was right. Now Doup got milk from Rossan's cow every day and all the food he could stuff himself with. Maybe she should let him stay here. But the mere thought of leaving him and being completely alone again caused tears to trickle slowly from her eyes.

"Well," said Foula, "it's not anything we can decide now. We have to talk to Rossan about it first."

Then she leaned over the spinning wheel and started it whirling, and shortly after, the Crow-Girl heard Eidi busying herself with the combing cards. But there was no consolation in those familiar sounds. Feeling heavy and tired, she lay under the hides and let her tears run freely down the pillow.

Rossan returned a couple of days later. He brought a wine-red silk ribbon for Eidi and a sky-blue one for the Crow-Girl, and for Foula he had various kinds of herb seeds. Doup received a music box. And Rossan had sugar and tea and a tin of tobacco for himself. He had managed to sell all the yarn, and people had praised its fine quality.

He talked about his trip at supper. He said that Foula's husband had been at the market and had gone around to customers asking about her and Eidi.

"He also came over to me," said Rossan, "for he had heard that I had people living here. But I said that it was two orphans whom I had met one evening when I was on my way home.

"I don't know if he believed me. He stood there

staring at the yarn. Then he said, 'Those children are truly good at spinning.' And I answered that the girl was big enough to be able to spin, but the boy was not yet big enough to be able to speak clearly. And, after all, that's not completely wrong," he said. Then he smiled at the Crow-Girl. "It's not good to have to lie, but it's good to be able to."

Rossan ate a few mouthfuls of soup, then looked at Foula and said, "Nevertheless I have the feeling that he could show up here. But it is also about the time when all of you wanted to be taking off anyway. And at Crow-Girl's cove you'll not be disturbed. I can scarcely believe that there is anyone who remembers the place anymore."

Foula opened her mouth as if she were about to say something but then closed it again.

Rossan leaned back in his chair, rubbing his paunch. Then he put his hands behind his head and looked around at the little flock. "It's been cozy having all of you living here. I think I'll miss you, but I'm an old hermit, you know. And one has to wonder if that's not what suits me best!"

13

A couple of days later Rossan took them out to the sheep, so they could each choose one.

"Foula, you're first," he said, "for you're the oldest."

Foula stood for a good bit of time looking at the flock. Then she chose a large light-gray sheep, which, by the way it bulged out on both sides, was obviously carrying a lamb in its belly.

Rossan nodded his approval. "She's a good choice, has fine wool, and always has twins."

"Baaa," bleated Doup at the flock from up in his basket on the horse's back.

Then it was the Crow-Girl's turn. But she shook her head and did not want any of them. "My sheep was the one the bog took."

Rossan did not pressure her but let Eidi choose one.

She immediately chose a white sheep with long silky wool.

Again Rossan nodded. "She is just a year old. A fine animal. Her mother also always has twins."

Then he looked inquiringly at the Crow-Girl, but she again shook her head. So with Glennie's help, they caught the two sheep and dragged them to the stable.

Once they were back home, Glennie immediately leapt into the basket with her two pups. They had already grown much larger and could easily be left alone while she was out with Rossan and the sheep.

The Crow-Girl sat down on the bed beside them and scratched them behind their ears. Rossan pulled a chair over and sat down by her.

"Well," he said, "Glennie is getting to be an old dog. Earlier she had five or six pups at a time. Now it may be that she'll have no more at all. I'd better keep one of them."

"What will happen to the other one?" the Crow-Girl wanted to know.

"Oh, well," said Rossan, "it will probably be hard to find a place for it. Would you consider taking it?"

The Crow-Girl looked up at him with eyes shining. Then she shook her head. "No," she said decidedly. "I was given a sheep. That must be enough."

"That's a pity," said Rossan. "I don't like having to kill it, but three dogs are too many for me."

"Kill it!" gasped the Crow-Girl. "Then you had better give it to me."

"I think that's a better idea, too. You'll need a dog for the sheep. Which one would you like?"

Both pups were females, and both were black. But one had a little white fan on its breast, and it was the one that the Crow-Girl pointed to.

"That's fine," said Rossan as he stood up and put his chair back in its place. "She's yours."

They made up a whole little flock on the morning they set out from Rossan's. Eidi pulled the two sheep behind her, and the Crow-Girl led the horse with Doup and the pup in the baskets. Foula walked in front, holding the pail of coals in one hand and a bundle in the other.

Rossan stood at the side of the road and watched them go. He would gladly have accompanied them to the cove, but he had no one to look after the animals.

At the curve in the road they all stopped, turned around, and waved. Rossan waved back.

Foula kept standing there.

"Come on now," called Eidi.

So they went on, and Rossan and Glennie disappeared from sight.

The Crow-Girl raised her head and looked around. The sea was no longer visible. The countryside lay bare and brown before her. But there was spring in the air. Flocks of birds came in long steady flights, and the wind felt warm against her face. She flared her nostrils, drawing the air deep into her lungs and catching the scent of grass.

Down between the dried blades along the road fresh green shoots pushed up their tips. Low willow bushes with downy catkins on their branches stood along the edge of the bogs. Chirping birds were flitting from one bush to another. The wind came alternately in quick blasts and gentle breaths; clouds rushed across the sky. The whole world was in motion.

For several days they kept to the road, until one day they came to a high cliff rising beside it. There a path turned off, and the Crow-Girl suggested that they take it.

Since it was the first path they had seen in several days, they decided to do so. Whether it led directly to the cove, they didn't know, but in any case it led toward the sea, and from there they could walk along the shore until they reached the cove.

The path was narrow and difficult. The two sheep had to be tied so that they walked one behind the other, for there was no room for them to walk side by side.

Slowly the group made headway. Then the Crow-Girl shouted, "Look, it's the sea!"

And far out, there was a shining strip of silver. Suddenly walking became easier with it in sight.

All day they followed the stony path, where the

sea seemed close by, and the hollows of the valleys, where it could not be seen. The ground was wet and difficult, their feet became stuck, and the ice-cold water seeped into their shoes.

Their shadows moved from beside them to behind them. Doup and the puppy fell asleep, each in a basket, and awoke again. The sun hung low and shone in their faces. The sea had turned bright blue.

They had been going upward for a long time and now reached the crest of a ridge. Foula went first, then stopped and waited. She had stepped off the path onto dry ground, and one after the other they all made their way up to her. The Crow-Girl came last with the horse behind her.

Down below lay the cove. The brook spread like a shining fan across the rocky shore. The little house stood out sharply white against the sky-blue sea, where the current was drawing great swirls in endless movement. A bird of prey repeated those circles in the sky, before it let itself be moved backward, in above the land.

Foula stepped over to the Crow-Girl and put an arm around her shoulders. "How beautiful it is here," she said.

The Crow-Girl nodded.

They started the climb down. The Crow-Girl went first, and she was going at such speed that she was almost stumbling on loose stones and sharp rocks. When she reached the end of the path, she let go of the horse, rushed over to the house, threw open the door, and ran into the room.

It was completely empty.

The settle and everything that had been in it were gone: the table and chairs, her two big goatskins, and all the kettles and pots and pans. The only thing that remained was the old swan wing she had used for sweeping in front of the hearth.

Then she ran into the larder. It was just as empty: only a smashed crock was left lying in one corner.

Foula and Eidi and Doup appeared in the doorway. "What in the world has happened?" asked Foula.

But the Crow-Girl could not say anything at all. She felt as if someone had hit her very hard. Paralyzed and silent, she stood in the middle of the room staring at the bare walls. Then she thought of the driftwood and rushed out of the house and around to the back.

All the firewood was gone.

Her whole body began to shake. She stamped her feet on the ground, and strange sounds forced their way out of her mouth. Her fists struck out at the empty air, because there was no one they could strike. She was so angry that she felt she might go to pieces.

"Thief," she then screamed. "And she called *me* a little thief! That thieving hag, that . . ."

For she was certain that it was the woman from the hamlet by the fjord who had been there with her husband. She stomped her cold, wet feet until her soles began to burn and her anger began to abate.

"It's shameful to take all of someone's worldly goods—not to mention stealing from a child," Foula said behind her. "But we don't know, after all, that it was they who did it, and even if we knew, it wouldn't help us just now. Done is done, and in a short while the sun will go down, so we had better gather some heather to sleep on. And some firewood. Eidi will look after Doup and the animals. Come on, we must get busy!"

Her voice was calm and determined.

The Crow-Girl let her fists fall and turned toward her. "Yes," she said, drying her eyes. "Let's get busy."

They worked hard, until it grew so dark they could no longer see a thing. But by then, a large bed had been made up in one corner of the room and a wet fire fizzed and sputtered on the hearth.

They each ate a hunk of bread and a piece of smoked mutton and went to bed exhausted.

Thus began their life at the cove.

14

The first thing Foula did was to start clearing a piece of ground for planting potatoes. She chose an area enclosed by a stone fence behind the house with the damaged roof.

They had placed the horse in the part of the house where the roof did not leak, and there Foula had found an old shovel and some other tools beneath the thick dust.

From early morning until late evening she dug her way through the head-high forest of ferns that had spread across the small field. And each time she had managed to clear a little part, she cut up a potato so that there was an eye on each piece and then placed the pieces in the ground.

Eidi and the Crow-Girl gathered firewood. They took the horse with them and walked along the shore, filling the baskets. Soon a long row of wood lay piled behind the house, just as there had been in earlier times.

The Crow-Girl also showed Eidi how to gather mussels and snails and to harvest sea kale. And it was not long before they could begin collecting seagull eggs, even if both were afraid of the screeching birds that dove down pointing their sharp beaks at their heads.

The sheep walked around at large, and a couple of times a day the Crow-Girl went out to look after them. She took along the pup, whom she had begun to call Glennie, and tried to teach that little black lump the calls that the old Glennie had obeyed. But the young Glennie was more concerned with dancing gnats and buzzing bees than with large animals.

Foula's sheep had twins, as Rossan had predicted, two small dark-brown lambs that tumbled along beside their mother to get a drop of milk.

Once in a while Foula went with the Crow-Girl

out to the ewe, and while the Crow-Girl held it, Foula milked a mug of milk for Doup, so that he could keep his round cheeks.

Eidi's sheep had her first lamb—a light-brown one with the finest curly wool. But it was male, so Foula hurried to warn her that at some point it would be butchered, just as one of her own would.

All the potatoes were eventually in the ground, and Foula was busy clearing room for the other vegetables. The hard work did not seem to bother her. She shook her head when the Crow-Girl offered to help.

"You have enough to look after," she said. "Driftwood and the sheep and all the things you go about gathering up. You're the one who's best at that. And I'm best with the soil. In earlier times I had the finest vegetable patch in the whole area. And I intend to have it again."

Then she had to laugh at the thought of where she was. "I'd like to know whom I should compare myself with."

They did not always have enough food, but they did not starve. They put mussels and seagull eggs in the warm ashes of the fire and each evening cut a small piece off the smoked mutton leg Rossan had given them. When the bone was plucked clean of every single shred of meat, Glennie got it to gnaw on.

After Foula had found the shovel, the Crow-Girl began hunting for things in the other house and in the ruin. Earlier she had never thought about who had lived in the two dwellings. They were just there, and always had been. But now she wished that she had asked her grandmother. Curious, she rummaged under piles of stone and old plaster and dust.

In the ruin she found her best loot, a rusty old iron pot, which she scoured clean with sand and, flush with victory, brought home. But there were also other good things—such as a chipped crock, a broken ladle that could still be used, and a dented pot lid.

In the house she found nothing other than the head of a hammer and a box of old nails.

Once in a while she walked up to the valley where her grandparents were buried. There, she would sit on a stone and look down toward the cove and enjoy the sight of smoke curling up from the chimney, the little flock of many-colored sheep scattered out across the slopes, the eagles circling high above, the green grass, the blue sky, and the green-blue sea.

—And, once in a great while, a pair of crows flying by.

One day she was sitting with Doup down by the brook, trying to teach him to wash his hands. He still did not like water.

"Look," she said, "you stick your hands in the water and then do like this." She rubbed her hands together.

Doup remained at a good distance from the brook and did the same with his dry hands.

The Crow-Girl began to laugh. "Yes, that's right, but you need water."

So she leaned down, took some water in her hands, and carried it over to Doup. Wetting his hands, she showed him once more how he should rub them together.

Doup looked as if he had a few misgivings, but he did it.

Then she took him by the hand and walked with

him along the stream, down toward the shore. Glennie came leaping behind with wagging tail and cheerful barks.

But before she reached the sea, she came to a stop. Two men were walking along the shore toward them. They had the sun at their backs so she could not see their faces, even when she shaded her eyes with her hand. But she could see that the larger of them had a gun on his back. And when they came closer, she could also see that the one with the gun was a grown man; the other was a boy a half a head taller than she, and he had a couple of ducks hanging over his shoulder.

When the two strangers had come nearly right up to them, the man stretched out his arms as if he wanted to pick up Doup. But Doup became frightened and ran over to the Crow-Girl.

"Mine Cwo," he called, and she lifted him up.

"Well, of course, he can't recognize me," said the man. "And I daresay you can't either."

He extended his hand to shake, and the Crow-Girl cautiously gave him hers, while she held Doup with her other arm.

"My name is Frid, and I am the boy's father." And

a pair of blue, blue eyes looked at her above a gray-flecked beard. His eyes still had a sorrowful tinge, but their empty, desperate look was gone. "And this is my older son, Ravnar."

The boy stepped forward and shook her hand. His eyes were just as blue as his father's, but his hair was dark.

"So we found you at last," said Frid.

The Crow-Girl was completely dumbfounded and did not know what to say. She just stood there holding Doup and staring at them.

Foula came running over from the field. Panting, she positioned herself beside the Crow-Girl and looked around as she tried to catch her breath.

"Who are you and what are you doing here?" she asked worriedly.

And Frid explained it all to her.

"Well, so you are Doup's father," she exclaimed with a sigh of relief.

"Doup, is that what you call him?"

The Crow-Girl nodded. "It was he himself who started it. I didn't know, of course, what his name was."

"It doesn't matter. If he is used to being called

Doup, let's just keep on doing so. I can't tell you how grateful I am that you have taken care of him, and particularly now when I can see how well he's doing. If there is anything I can do in return, you must tell me."

The Crow-Girl could not nod, for Doup had gotten hold of her braid and was clutching it tightly.

"Little scamp, let go," she said, and forced his hand open. Then she put him down on the ground.

"You must need to sit down," said Foula. "Come over to the house; we have a bench outdoors there. But indoors there are only beds and the bare floor to sit on."

They led Frid and Ravnar to the bench and seated themselves on a couple of large stones that they had dragged over for that very purpose. Eidi came out of the house and greeted them in surprise.

Then Frid said that Ravnar, who had been herding sheep for a relative, had come home one day and found him in the ruined house, and that they had gone out together to search for Doup and the Crow-Girl.

And the Crow-Girl told about her whole journey from the cove and back again.

15

When the sun began to set, they went into the house, and Foula roasted the two ducks at the hearth.

That night Frid and Ravnar slept in the attic. Foula and the Crow-Girl had made up a new bed for Doup and the Crow-Girl, and Foula and Eidi slept together in the old one.

After everyone had gone to bed and the coals were banked, the Crow-Girl lay awake for a long time. Doup lay sucking his thumb, and the Crow-Girl, fumbling for him in the dark, struck something cold and hard. She cautiously lifted the music box from his hands and, finding his head, stroked his hair.

He stopped sucking, but when she took away her hand, he immediately began again.

This time there was nothing to be done. Frid would take Doup with him, and she would perhaps never see him again. The Crow-Girl could scarcely bear the thought, but she had to mull it over in order to find a way out. And before she fell asleep, she felt she might have, just maybe, come up with something—but it depended on Frid.

The next morning she crept out of bed while the others slept. She threw the shawl about her and walked barefoot down to the brook, where she seated herself on the flat stone that jutted out into the water.

She took a handful of the ice-cold water and splashed it over her face. Then she took a deep breath and looked around her.

Across the land the sun was about to rise behind a veil of light clouds. The sheep were grazing on the slope, and down by the stony shore she caught sight of Frid. She got up and walked over to him.

"It's a lovely place you have here," he said.

"Yes, and that's why I have something I want to ask you about."

Frid looked at her.

"Yesterday you said that if there was something you could do for me, I should just say so."

He nodded.

"Stay here!"

"Stay here?" He looked at her amazed, then turned his head and stared out across the sea. "You are very fond of Doup?" he said quietly.

The Crow-Girl nodded.

"I'll talk to Ravnar about it," he said. "I can't simply say yes just like that. You surely understand?"

The Crow-Girl nodded again.

"I'll give you an answer by this evening," said Frid. "I must use the day to think about it. It's a big decision. But we'll be here for a couple of days at least."

The Crow-Girl spun round on her heel, ran back along the brook, and sat down on the stone.

How dumb she was! Of course he wouldn't agree to it. He had his own place with his own stable and his own fields lying right next to the main road. Why would he want to be out here in this wilderness?

She wiped her nose with the back of her hand and washed her face once more before she got up and returned to the house.

Foula had lit a fire in the hearth and was making soup from the bones of the two ducks. Doup and Glennie were rolling around on the floor, and Eidi, having trouble waking up, lay rubbing her eyes.

The Crow-Girl went over to Foula.

"I asked Frid to stay here," she said to her.

"Well, that was a good idea," said Foula. "Then we wouldn't need to be parted from Doup. Did he want to?"

The Crow-Girl shook her head. "I don't think so. He'll give me an answer before evening."

Foula put her arm around her. "You poor dear," she merely said. And the Crow-Girl pressed her face in against Foula's body.

They ate breakfast sitting out on the bench and on the stones around it. The soup was good and warm and filled with small pieces of meat that Foula had painstakingly picked from the bones.

"How delightful it is to have some meat," said Foula.

"Maybe I should get some more," said Frid. "Is there any game around here?"

The Crow-Girl nodded. "There are wild goats and seals and all kinds of birds here."

"Seals!" exclaimed Ravnar. "I'd really like to see them. I've never seen a seal."

"I can take you out with me and show them to you," suggested the Crow-Girl.

"That would be great!"

"I think I'll go out after a goat," said Frid, "even if they are difficult to get close to." Then he turned to Doup. "What do you say, little Doup? Wouldn't you like to have a goatskin to lie on?"

But Doup just stared at him with large eyes before hurrying over to the Crow-Girl and crawling up on her lap.

The water softly gurgled back and forth between the rocks.

Ravnar and the Crow-Girl sat completely still watching the seals, which, one after another, slid into the pool in order to swim farther out toward the open sea. For a moment, one of them positioned itself upright in the water and looked at them before following the others.

"Did you see that?" exclaimed Ravnar. "It looked straight into our eyes."

The Crow-Girl nodded.

Without thinking about it, she had sat gathering beach snails from the stones just beneath the water's surface. Now she opened her hand and let the small dark-gray snail shells disappear into the depths because she remembered that Frid might manage to shoot a goat.

"I have suggested to your father that all of you stay here."

Ravnar nodded. "Yes, so he said. I hope that he will agree. There are all too many memories tied to our own house. I think that if I had not come home, he would have gone mad. It was completely smashed, windows and everything." He looked at her. "But, of course, you know that. I had to plug the holes in the panes with old pillows and blankets, so that we wouldn't freeze to death. And I couldn't get him to say what had happened—only that my mother was dead and that he had sent Doup off with you."

The Crow-Girl could see that his eyes had begun to glisten and that his mouth quivered a tiny bit. She sat completely still so that he would not burst into tears.

His gaze was empty and far out across the sea. Then he took a deep breath and continued. "It was not until we were on the way here that he said she had fallen into the bog."

He stared blankly again, letting his glance slide out toward the horizon. An eagle screeched above their heads. And the water prattled among the stones.

"There's a large bog in the heath that stretches up to our house," he said.

The Crow-Girl nodded.

"He was so used to going hunting out there that I think he had totally forgotten how dangerous it could be. Then one day he took my mother and Doup along to gather berries."

"Doup!" exclaimed the Crow-Girl.

"Yes, he was sitting on my father's shoulders. It was then that my mother slipped and . . ." Ravnar hid his face in his hands and allowed himself to cry. Great sobs rose up from his very depths and made his shoulders shake.

The Crow-Girl cautiously laid her hand on his

back and held it there until he stopped crying. When he lifted his head, she removed her hand.

He dried his eyes with his knuckles. They sat for a long while looking out across the sea.

Then the Crow-Girl got up. "Come on, let's go back."

Later in the afternoon Frid appeared on the crest of the hill with a young billy goat across his shoulders. It had taken him the better part of the day to get into shooting distance of it.

He skinned and cleaned it on the flat stone in the brook, and Foula promised to care for the skin so Doup would have it to sleep on.

Frid cut off a leg for dinner, and the rest of the carcass was hung up in the attic.

The Crow-Girl sat on the bench outside the house and followed him with her eyes, especially when he and Ravnar went down to the shore together.

The sun was about to set out across the sea, and the two figures stood like black silhouettes against the pink clouds and the glowing sun. They talked for a long time.

At last, black spots began to dance before the Crow-Girl's eyes, and she closed them to make the spots go away.

When she opened her eyes again, Frid and Ravnar were standing before her. Ravnar smiled at her, and Frid said, "We would be pleased to accept your invitation."

16

The Crow-Girl suggested to Frid that he repair the empty house, the house they used as a stable for the horse. But Frid wanted to fix it up for Foula and Eidi.

"One day, you will surely want to have your own house. And Eidi will, too," he said. "So Ravnar and I will take the ruin. And then Doup can join us later, when he is prepared to do so," he added a little sorrowfully, for Doup had not yet been willing to let Frid pick him up.

A couple of days later Frid and Ravnar set off for the town that lay farther up the main road. There, Frid would sell his house and land, and for the money he would buy lumber, lime, and mortar and have it all transported down the coast to the cove.

When they returned by the boat that was carrying their goods for them, it became apparent that Frid had gotten a good price for his place. There had been enough money to buy all kinds of things.

In addition to the materials for the houses, there had been sufficient money for a little plow that the horse could pull, a sack of oats, and a sack of potatoes.

For Doup he had bought a pair of woolen trousers, and for Eidi, Foula, and the Crow-Girl he had bought each a piece of cloth for a dress. Eidi's was light brown with a gold-leaf pattern; Foula's was a subdued apple-green with small red berries with dark-green stems; and the Crow-Girl's was sky-blue with white feathers sprinkled all over it.

But the best of all was the furniture he gave the Crow-Girl in thanks for her having taken such good care of Doup, and as a sort of payment for entrusting him with the ruin and the fields around it.

There were two settles of light, varnished wood, each as yellow and shiny as honey and with flowering vines and birds carved into a border along the back; a large dining table with two benches; and two chairs with slatted backs and arms in the same shiny yellow wood.

The Crow-Girl was filled with such joy when she saw it all that she threw her arms around Frid's waist. Doup, who wanted to join in, threw his arms around his legs. And Frid laughed.

In the evening they sat around the table eating the stew Foula had boiled up from some of the goat meat and some of the potatoes Frid had brought.

"How good it tastes," said Ravnar, sighing with satisfaction, as he took his third helping.

"Make sure to enjoy it, because it will be a long time before you get potatoes again," said Frid. "The rest must go into the ground. There's just enough time left. And then it'll be a while before we see a potato again."

"Not at all," said Foula with a smile, "for mine are already about to flower."

"Yum," said Eidi, because she loved new potatoes.

"I think Ravnar and I will begin with the land and then later fix up the houses—if we may live in the attic until then?" said Frid, looking at the Crow-Girl.

She nodded with her mouth full of food. Doup began to nod in the same way, and they all had to laugh.

Just at that moment the door was thrown open. A large, heavy man with a full red beard and a broad woman with a little gray knot of hair on top of her head stood in the doorway.

"What are you doing here?" the woman shrieked. "Don't you realize that this is private property?"

The Crow-Girl leapt up from the bench.

"Private property!" she shouted. "You bet your life it is! *My* property, that's exactly what it is. And don't you ever come here and steal from me again!"

Doup became frightened and started to cry. Eidi lifted him to her lap and started consoling him.

Frid, Ravnar, and Foula had also risen, and they all had their hands on the knives in their belts.

The man and his wife, dumbfounded, remained standing just inside the door.

Frid walked over and placed himself in front of them.

"Well, you're here at last," he said, and to the

Crow-Girl's surprise he sounded nearly friendly. "You've been a rather long time in coming to settle accounts for the furnishings, not to mention the driftwood, but . . ."

"Driftwood," snapped the woman. "Everyone has a right to gather that."

"Yes, in the place where one lives," said Frid, and his voice took on a slightly harsher tone; "otherwise, it counts as theft. But that, of course, is not the case here, for I can see that you have brought the money along."

He had pulled the knife up from his belt and was pointing it at the heavy leather pouch hanging from the man's belt. The man began to loosen it.

"Don't you do it!" the woman yelled.

Frid continued in a calm voice. "There is, after all, the possibility that we'll report it."

The man had gotten the pouch free and handed it to Frid. Frid took it and handed it to the Crow-Girl.

The woman stepped slightly closer, and now her voice had completely changed. "You surely haven't the heart to do that, have you now, little Crow-Girl," she fawned. "After everything we have done for you?

Didn't you get all you could eat, a good fire to sit by, and a bed to sleep in?"

The Crow-Girl nodded, but she hugged the pouch to her. At the woman's words, she began to itch all over her body, and she did not dare to let go of the money in order to scratch.

"For heaven's sake, just stop it!" shouted Frid. "First you let her toil and drudge for you, then you steal everything she has, and now you tell her that she owes you thanks. Get out!" He was so furious that his words cut through the air like the crack of a whip, and his eyes flashed icily blue.

"There is no harm in teaching children gratitude," said the woman, aggrieved. "We had planned to take her in as our own. You can be sure we're good people. We just wanted to look after her things, so that no one would steal . . ."

"OUT!" bellowed Frid.

And the woman and the man dared not do anything but turn around and hurry out the door.

"Such an ungrateful, thieving child" was the last they heard from the woman before the door slammed shut with a bang.

The Crow-Girl put the pouch down on the table and started to scratch herself. "Ugh," she said. "That woman always gets my entire body to itching."

"What awful people they are," said Foula, and sat down.

Frid was still so angry that his hands were trembling. "If she had been able to steal this house, I'm sure she would have taken it along, too," he said. He placed his hands on the tabletop to keep them still. "Gratitude," he snorted. Then he tossed his head as if to shake off his anger. "Now, Crow-Girl, let's see what they've paid you for what they took."

The Crow-Girl opened the pouch, and a whole handful of gold coins rolled out on the table.

"Hurray!" shouted Eidi. "Now you are rich."

"Hooway!" shouted Doup, and clapped his hands.

"What a lot of money," said Ravnar.

"Now you can buy anything you want," said Foula.

"I know what I would like the most," said the Crow-Girl.

"What is that?" asked Frid.

"A gun."

"A gun?" said Foula, surprised.

"Yes," said the Crow-Girl. "For if a person can

hunt, there's never any need to go hungry." Then she looked at Frid. "Will you teach me how?"

"You can count on it."

The Crow-Girl gave each of the others a gold coin so they could buy whatever they wanted for themselves, and the rest she hid up in the chimney behind a loose stone.

The next time Frid and Ravnar went into town, they bought a spinning wheel, three plump brown hens, and a rooster for Foula; a loom and two combing cards for Eidi; a cow for Doup, so that he would always have round cheeks; a sheep and twelve small windowpanes for Frid; and a gun for Ravnar and one for the Crow-Girl.

In the course of the summer Frid taught them how to hunt: to walk up against the wind and to sneak up on their prey, to wait for hours in hiding by a ford, and to skin and cut up the animals they had shot. And Foula showed them how to tan the skins.

They soon became good at hunting both deer and goats, but the Crow-Girl liked best of all to walk along the shore alone to shoot ducks.

Glennie proved to be a good hunting dog. When

the Crow-Girl shot a duck out over the water, Glennie swam out to get it, carefully carrying it in her mouth back to land.

But the Crow-Girl never went hunting out by the seals' pool, and she never fired a shot when there was a crow nearby.

17

Foula's potatoes were the first to flower, then Frid's. The oats stood rustling in their field, first green and later yellow. Parsnips and carrots waved their feathery tips in the wind. The kale grew tall and crinkly, and the lambs as large as sheep, and Doup's arms were growing out of the sleeves of his sweater.

The ruin had become a house, which, along with the stable Frid had built for the cow and the horse, stood shining bright white against the green grass and the gray rocks.

The empty house was no longer empty. Frid had repaired the roof, and Foula and Eidi had whitewashed it both inside and out. And afterward they had whitewashed the Crow-Girl's.

One fall day the Crow-Girl was sitting on the bench outside the house cleaning carrots and potatoes. Glennie, with her head on her front paws, lay dozing in the warm sunshine by the girl's feet.

There was a dead calm, and the smoke from the three chimneys was curling straight up into the sky. Foula was busy cleaning the whitewash off the windowpanes of her and Eidi's house. Eidi was over in the kitchen garden gathering in the last potatoes. A brown hen and a flock of half-grown chickens were scurrying around between Eidi's feet, searching for worms and other little creatures in the black dirt.

Doup was at Frid and Ravnar's. He was walking around with a hammer that Frid had made from the hammerhead the Crow-Girl had found in the ruin, and he was beating on everything that he came close to. Frid was busy making a table and some benches out of the wood that had been left over from the construction. Ravnar was helping him, and Doup believed that he was, too. The sheep were grazing along the banks of the brook.

The Crow-Girl sat enjoying the sight of the little group of houses. They almost resembled a real hamlet, she thought, with the smoke from the chimneys and all the people and animals.

Then she saw a figure approaching them by the inland path. She shaded her eyes with her hand and saw a pointed cap on top of a small, round person.

"Rossan!" she shouted, running with Glennie to meet him.

Eidi had also recognized him and came running over the plank across the brook. They reached him simultaneously, and he threw an arm around each of them.

"Such a welcome," he said.

And then they all began to talk at the same time, telling about everything that had happened since they parted from him.

"There, there," said Rossan laughing. "One at a time."

"Who is looking after your sheep?" the Crow-Girl wanted to know.

"My sister's next oldest boy came by to see if there was anything he could help me with. So I thought I would use the opportunity to see how all of you were. And fortunately you all seem to be just fine."

Foula came running, while drying her hands on her apron, and she and Rossan embraced. At last Frid and Ravnar and Doup came.

Glennie barked, and everyone talked, and suddenly Eidi shouted in order to drown them all out. "Now we're going to have a party. We'll butcher my male lamb."

That is what they did, or, more precisely, that is what Rossan and Foula did, while Eidi hid inside the house.

They placed the legs on a spit over the Crow-Girl's hearth and put a lot of big potatoes in the hot ashes. And in the evening they ate at her shiny yellow table, with Rossan at one end and the Crow-Girl at the other.

Frid sat beside the Crow-Girl with Doup on his lap and cut up small bits of meat for him. Fat was running down Doup's chin as he stuffed in the pieces faster than he could chew them.

"Now, now," said Frid. "Take it easy, there's food enough."

After a while they all began to eat more slowly.

"By the way, I ran into your husband the last time I was at the market," said Rossan to Foula. "I don't think you need fear his showing up. He has found a woman that he makes the rounds with at every single market for miles about, and they both drink, I daresay, the same amount."

The Crow-Girl glanced over at Foula to see if she was saddened by it, but she just smiled and looked relieved.

"I'm glad to hear it," she said.

Eidi nodded.

As they went on talking, the Crow-Girl sat regarding them:

Foula, who with reddened cheeks was smiling at Frid;

Frid, who was smiling back above Doup's head and who told her that this was the best roast lamb he had ever tasted;

Doup, who had finally had his fill and was now playing horse with a piece of meat, trotting it across the plate and out onto the table, while he made clicking noises with his tongue;

Eidi, who was still gnawing on a bone and had apparently forgotten all about its having been a part of her own light-brown male lamb;

Rossan with his neat beard, who was talking eagerly with Ravnar;

Ravnar, who again and again pushed a dark forelock away from his eyes.

She looked about the room—over in the corner at the broad bed that was entirely covered with goatskins, where she and Doup slept together; at the shadows that in the light of the fire were dancing on the newly whitewashed walls; at the light that was reflected in the honey-yellow wood of the settle, so the birds and flowers across the back looked as if they were moving.

"Look at her eyes," said Rossan.

It dawned on the Crow-Girl that they were all looking at her.

She was sitting at the end of the table and wearing the new dress Foula had sewn for her. White feathers floated down on the sky-blue fabric, and the sleeves reached all the way to her wrists. Her hair was black and shiny, and the silk ribbon that Rossan had once given her could be seen in blue glimpses down through the braid at her back. At the end of it hung a

black-and-gray crow's feather. And her eyes! They were gleaming dark blue, nearly black, beneath her dark brows.

"I think we should toast Crow-Girl," said Frid, "for it's owing to her that we are together."

They lifted their mugs and toasted her, and she could feel that her eyes began to glisten and her cheeks grow warm.

When Frid had put down his mug again, he said, "Tell me something. Wasn't 'Crow-Girl' what that horrible woman from the hamlet by the fjord called you?"

The Crow-Girl nodded. "Well, she said that I resembled one, and so I said that that was my name. She continued to ask what my name was, and that was the only one I could come up with."

"But isn't there something else you would rather be called?" Frid asked.

"I don't know what it would be," she said.

"Mine Cwo, *mine*," called Doup, stretching his arms out toward her.

She lifted him onto her lap, and he threw his arms around her before she could manage to dry the fat off his fingers. "How about Myna?" she asked.

"Myna," Doup said, delighted.

"Then that's what I will be called," the Crow-Girl said with a big smile. "Myna."

"It seems that Doup has helped you find a name, just as you found one for him," said Foula.

"A toast to Myna," said Rossan, and stood up. The others did the same.

When they had sat down again, Ravnar said, "I think it's a shame if we completely forget 'Crow-Girl,' so what do all of you say to our calling the place here Crow Cove?"

He looked at Myna, and she nodded. She was glad that the crows were not to be forgotten.

"Crow Cove," said Eidi. "It's a wonderful name."

And so they toasted again.

The stone beneath Myna's feet felt smooth and cold, and curving around it, the brook murmured on. The sea's waves softly licked the shore, and from her house came the sounds of happy voices.

The moon shone on the little cove and made the three houses stand out brightly white against the dark stone cliffs. Myna made a hollow of her hand and leaned down to drink a sip of the clear icy water.

black-and-gray crow's feather. And her eyes! They were gleaming dark blue, nearly black, beneath her dark brows.

"I think we should toast Crow-Girl," said Frid, "for it's owing to her that we are together."

They lifted their mugs and toasted her, and she could feel that her eyes began to glisten and her cheeks grow warm.

When Frid had put down his mug again, he said, "Tell me something. Wasn't 'Crow-Girl' what that horrible woman from the hamlet by the fjord called you?"

The Crow-Girl nodded. "Well, she said that I resembled one, and so I said that that was my name. She continued to ask what my name was, and that was the only one I could come up with."

"But isn't there something else you would rather be called?" Frid asked.

"I don't know what it would be," she said.

"Mine Cwo, *mine*," called Doup, stretching his arms out toward her.

She lifted him onto her lap, and he threw his arms around her before she could manage to dry the fat off his fingers. "How about Myna?" she asked.

"Myna," Doup said, delighted.

"Then that's what I will be called," the Crow-Girl said with a big smile. "Myna."

"It seems that Doup has helped you find a name, just as you found one for him," said Foula.

"A toast to Myna," said Rossan, and stood up. The others did the same.

When they had sat down again, Ravnar said, "I think it's a shame if we completely forget 'Crow-Girl,' so what do all of you say to our calling the place here Crow Cove?"

He looked at Myna, and she nodded. She was glad that the crows were not to be forgotten.

"Crow Cove," said Eidi. "It's a wonderful name."

And so they toasted again.

The stone beneath Myna's feet felt smooth and cold, and curving around it, the brook murmured on. The sea's waves softly licked the shore, and from her house came the sounds of happy voices.

The moon shone on the little cove and made the three houses stand out brightly white against the dark stone cliffs. Myna made a hollow of her hand and leaned down to drink a sip of the clear icy water.

black-and-gray crow's feather. And her eyes! They were gleaming dark blue, nearly black, beneath her dark brows.

"I think we should toast Crow-Girl," said Frid, "for it's owing to her that we are together."

They lifted their mugs and toasted her, and she could feel that her eyes began to glisten and her cheeks grow warm.

When Frid had put down his mug again, he said, "Tell me something. Wasn't 'Crow-Girl' what that horrible woman from the hamlet by the fjord called you?"

The Crow-Girl nodded. "Well, she said that I resembled one, and so I said that that was my name. She continued to ask what my name was, and that was the only one I could come up with."

"But isn't there something else you would rather be called?" Frid asked.

"I don't know what it would be," she said.

"Mine Cwo, *mine*," called Doup, stretching his arms out toward her.

She lifted him onto her lap, and he threw his arms around her before she could manage to dry the fat off his fingers. "How about Myna?" she asked.

"Myna," Doup said, delighted.

"Then that's what I will be called," the Crow-Girl said with a big smile. "Myna."

"It seems that Doup has helped you find a name, just as you found one for him," said Foula.

"A toast to Myna," said Rossan, and stood up. The others did the same.

When they had sat down again, Ravnar said, "I think it's a shame if we completely forget 'Crow-Girl,' so what do all of you say to our calling the place here Crow Cove?"

He looked at Myna, and she nodded. She was glad that the crows were not to be forgotten.

"Crow Cove," said Eidi. "It's a wonderful name."

And so they toasted again.

The stone beneath Myna's feet felt smooth and cold, and curving around it, the brook murmured on. The sea's waves softly licked the shore, and from her house came the sounds of happy voices.

The moon shone on the little cove and made the three houses stand out brightly white against the dark stone cliffs. Myna made a hollow of her hand and leaned down to drink a sip of the clear icy water.

Then she dried her hand on her forehead, cooling her skin.

The night air came pushing in, and together with it came a feeling that a great wish had been fulfilled, that in some strange way she had gotten what she had hoped for. And for a dizzying moment she felt perfectly happy.

She drew a deep breath and put her head back, and there, high up in the sky, she saw the North Star winking down at her.

She sat there until she began to be chilly; then she got up and walked back to the warm house.